The
Young
Healer

The
Young
Healer

Frank N. McMillan III

Mackinac Island Press

for the love of reading

A Mackinac Island Book
Published by Charlesbridge
85 Main Street
Watertown, MA 02472
(617) 926-0329
www.charlesbridge.com

Library of Congress Cataloging-in-Publication Data on file
Fiction
ISBN 978-1-934133-49-1 (hardcover)
ISBN 978-1-934133-50-7 (paperback)

Summary: Eleven-year-old Feather Anderson discovers her Lakota heritage with her grandfather and in doing so follows in his footsteps of becoming a medicine healer.

Printed February 2014 by Worzalla Publishing Company in Stevens Point, Wisconsin, USA
(hc) 10 9 8 7 6 5 4 3 2 1
(sc) 10 9 8 7 6 5 4 3 2

DEDICATION

This story is dedicated to the First Americans, in all their many nations and peoples, down to every generation, in profound respect for, and in appreciation of, their historical spiritual wisdom and moral bravery in declaring to the world that all created beings on Mother Earth— her two-legged, four-legged, and winged children, and her forests, mountains and rivers—are one family.

Frank N. McMillan III

The National Association of Elementary School Principals Children's Book of the Year Contest winner is carefully selected by a panel of national book experts. *The Young Healer* is a chapter book winner. It is a unique tale that will capture the imaginations of young and old.

CHAPTER ONE

*M*y name is Feather. Yes, that's my real name. It was given to me by my grandfather, my "tunkashila," as the Old Ones still say. His name is Spotted Eagle. Grandfather is Lakota. So is my mother, Ann Yellow Horse. Some history books call the Lakota people the Sioux Indians. Grandfather doesn't especially like that. He says "Sioux" is only a made-up name. According to him he's Lakota, pure and simple, a member of the Lakota nation, an Oglala—One of the People.

My father's name is William Hughes Anderson. And he's from Massachusetts, which makes me half Lakota and half whatever people from Massachusetts are, I guess. I have Mom's straight, dark hair and Dad's green eyes. And I'm tall for my age, like Dad. My full name is Feather Frances Anderson. Feather is not a bad sort of name; it's just, you know, different. The kids at school are finally used to it. It took them awhile—believe me.

All the way to third grade. Now I think they kind of like it. I know I do. I'm proud of my name.

Dad doesn't live with us anymore. He moved out the summer after my little brother, Peter, was born. Then came the divorce. That was four years ago. I was seven. I still see him . . . sometimes. He's an anthropology professor at a college outside of Boston, but he doesn't come back to New York very often. Usually he's working in the Amazonian rain forest or someplace like that. Mom says he always runs away.

To tell the truth I do have another name besides Feather, but I can't tell anyone what it is. At least not yet. Grandfather also gave it to me. Not long ago, in fact. It's a special Lakota name. Usually Grandfather just calls me "Takoja," which means grandchild. I'm not supposed to tell anybody my new name until I'm older. I'm not exactly sure of the reason why, but Grandfather's pretty insistent about it. And he ought to know. He's a medicine man.

Mom's an attorney and very practical. And she sure doesn't go by her real Lakota name. She opted for just plain Ann Anderson. She says Grandfather is too old-fashioned. But I don't think so. He just thinks differently—in a good way. And he's done things most people don't even dream about. He lives in the spare bedroom in our apartment and he always tells me stories. I love him a lot. He's over eighty years old. Exactly how old, I don't know. He doesn't know either. He says the government didn't keep very good records on the reservations back in the old days.

Grandfather says he was born on a winter morning so cold that water froze inside his parents' cabin. That's cold. He also says people have it easy nowadays. When he was a boy, his "kunshi" (his great grandma) told him that when she was small, the Lakota people often had to eat their own moccasins or tree bark when the snow was deep and the buffalo were scarce. I can't imagine ever being that hungry!

Grandfather has lots of stories. Most are happy, but some are sad, like the one about his own grandfather, Iron Crow, who was killed by the soldiers at the place called Wounded Knee on a day when the ice was thick and the ponies were starving. Iron Crow was outside his lodge fighting to protect the helpless ones—the elders and young children—when the soldiers shot him. Grandfather's voice gets all gravelly when he tells that story. It makes me sad, too, especially the part about the children. I wish I'd known Iron Crow. I don't think there are too many people like him around anymore, except maybe for Grandfather.

I'm typing this on my laptop in my room. Grandfather told me it was important to tell stories, even if no one was listening. "Tell it to yourself, then." So I am. It's not like I have tons else to do right now, because I'm only allowed ten minutes of phone time a day since Mom took away my internet privileges. Texting and Facebook are totally off limits for the time being, too. The truth is I've been severely grounded because my friend Emily and I cut class the other day, and Mom caught us! But that was because I thought I saw Mrs. Green, this wonderful strange character I met with Grandfather that morning my brother was so sick that they took him to the hospital when, well, Grandfather and I played "hooky" as Mom calls it. And when I told her that it was just that the mysterious Mrs. Green was a major part of everything that happened that day, all she said was "I don't want to hear it."

Mom said grounding me hurts her more than it hurts me. Yeah, well, that's her opinion. Mine's a little different. And she also said that while she loved me and was proud of what Grandfather and I did that day, I still had to learn a lesson about skipping school.

Personally I prefer to think of it as an adventure Grandfather and I had—or better, a quest. Actually Grandfather said we went on a vision quest, just like young Lakota warriors did in the old days when they ventured out alone into the wilderness. In a way I suppose that's what we did, except you could say we went on a modern-day vision quest right in the heart of New York City.

It's not really a long story. Basically we went shopping, ate pizza, rode in a magic taxi, talked to a bear at the Central Park Zoo, did an ancient tribal ceremony on top of the Empire State Building, snuck into my brother's hospital room, and healed him as he lay dying. Nothing to it. And along the way, we met a bunch of awesome people, including Mrs. Green, and a few who were . . . well, let's just say they were a little less awesome.

It all started last week on a typical, boring school day, a typical, boring morning that led to the most amazing day of my life. The day they said I saved my brother's life. The day I got my new name. My new "secret" name.

CHAPTER TWO

*I*t was second period math class. While Mrs. Ortega was writing on the chalkboard, my friend Emily, who sits right across from me, slipped me a note. Emily is absolutely famous for her notes. She folded this one extra tight, so it was obviously important, I remember thinking, as I gently pried it open. Rustling paper always puts Mrs. Ortega on high alert. She has the hearing of a golden retriever and, man, is she serious about passing notes. If she finds one of those going around—or, worse, catches you sending a text—well, let's just say her bite is worse than her bark. Needless to say we're always careful . . . not that we don't keep doing it. Nobody likes a quitter, right?

"Well?" Emily said with her eyes.

I read the note: "This is top secret. Repete, top secret." I laughed to myself. Emily never was the greatest speller.

I kept reading. "What are you doing after school? I heard Billy Braslau is going to be at Banzai Pizza with some friends. I think he really likes you. Seriously. Let's go there and aksidently "bump" into him. You can call your mom when my mom picks us up. This is important, E."

As quietly as I could, I tore a piece of paper from my ring binder. Emily nearly died when I ripped it out. Her black perm bounced with nervous energy. I bet if you hooked Emily up to a generator, you could power all of New York City and large parts of Jersey. Luckily Mrs. Ortega's supersensitive ears didn't detect a thing. She was completely absorbed in explaining numerators and denominators.

My pencil was dull, so my answer was kind of sloppy. "Are you sure? You better be, 'cause if—"

Someone knocked on the door. Thankful for the distraction, the whole class turned toward the noise as fast as my cat Miko does to the sound of the electric can opener. I stopped writing and shoved the note inside my math book. The school counselor, Mr. Jenkins, stuck his shiny, bald head inside the room. He whispered to Mrs. Ortega, and then they both stared so hard in my direction that it felt like their eyes pierced holes right through me.

Mrs. Ortega cleared her throat. "Feather?"

"Yes, ma'am?" I was really self-conscious now because everyone was looking at me.

"Could you step outside for a moment, please?"

The whole class gasped, "Oooh!" My heart started to beat fast.

"And bring your belongings, too, please," Mrs. Ortega added.

"Oooh!" went the class.

My heart really started to thump. 'What did I do now?' I wondered. I pulled on my coat and backpack. I was halfway down the aisle when I remembered I'd left my mittens and hat under my desk, so I rushed back to get them. The whole class was staring at me like I was going to the electric chair or something. I heard somebody snicker mockingly at the back of the room.

Emily twisted around in her seat, looking all panicky, and mouthed the words "Call me!" She lives for emergencies. I nodded at her and ran back to the door.

I realized at that moment I wasn't in trouble after all when I got a better look at the expression on Mrs. Ortega's face up close. She looked worried, not mad. "Feather, honey, apparently there's an illness in your family. Someone's coming to pick you up. Why don't you wait in the office? Mr. Jenkins will go with you."

An illness. My little brother, Peter! It couldn't be my grandfather, who was out of town visiting relatives back on the reservation, and, as far as I knew, he'd never been sick a day in his life. Off and on for weeks, though, Peter had run a high fever. Nobody could figure out what was causing it. One doctor said it was a rare virus; another said, no, it was some kind of low-grade infection. To be honest nobody knew what was wrong. Mom had dragged him to nearly every specialist in Manhattan, but nothing seemed to help. Normally a superactive, five-year-old boy, always jumping and laughing in front of his favorite video game or begging to go to the park, Peter had been all listless and dazed lately. Sometimes he didn't even want to get off the sofa to eat. Mom was freaking out.

Mr. Jenkins walked down the hall with me. "Feather, I don't want you to worry," he said in a phony, concerned tone of voice, the kind adults use when they don't want you to get scared. "I'll see that all your assignments are taken care of."

Great. Wouldn't want to miss any assignments. Who cared about homework? That was about the last thing on my mind. Had my little brother gotten worse now? Then suddenly I thought about my mother. Did something happen to her? What if she was sick?

Mr. Jenkins steered me to the smelly, avocado-colored vinyl couch outside the principal's office. "Would you like me to sit here with you, Feather? Would you like to talk? You might feel better."

"No thanks, Mr. Jenkins. I'll be okay, really."

He stared at me like he didn't believe me. Mr. Jenkins thought people always wanted to talk. Talking was his job, I guess. He watched me like I was about to have a nervous breakdown or something. I knew he was just trying to be helpful. Still, I sure hoped he would leave . . . and soon.

"I'm fine, Mr. Jenkins. I promise." I started fiddling around in my backpack like I was looking for something. I thought maybe if I ignored him, he'd get the hint and leave. Thankfully, he did.

"Remember, I'm right down the hall if you need me. Okay?"

"Okay, thanks." When his office door shut, I let out a big sigh. He's a nice guy and all, but he's kind of weird. He still wears bell-bottoms, if that tells you anything.

I sat on the couch and stared at a water stain on the ceiling. I decided that if I had to wait there, I'd just put everything out of my mind until they came and got me. The school office was definitely a busy place. Phones kept ringing, teachers kept going in and out, and, in a few minutes, a seventh-grade guy I didn't know was coming in with a bloody nose that was squirting blood all over the place like a geyser. Even old Mrs. Bronsky, the school nurse who'd been in the Army for like a million years, looked like she was going to puke. It was awesome in a gross sort of way.

I didn't have to wait too long. I was digging in my purse, mining for some gum, when the street door opened, letting in a blast of cold air. All of a sudden, Mrs. Lewis the school secretary sucked wind like a sick Hoover. I raised my head to see who was there.

Grandfather! I fumbled my purse in surprise, as a tube of Mom-forbidden, hot-pink lip gloss rolled across the floor. I couldn't believe my eyes! "Tunkashila! What are you doing here?" I shouted for joy. "I thought you were in South Dakota!"

Grandfather rubbed his hands together and blew on them. Then he gave me a big smile. "I was. I left last night on the red-eye flight." He put his hand on my shoulder. "Peter was admitted to the hospital this morning. I'm here to collect you. We have a mission."

"C-Collect me? Why? What's going on? What happened? Is he going to be all right?"

He winked like he had a secret. "I'll tell you everything in good time, Takoja." He picked up the runaway lip gloss and handed it to me. Then he kissed the top of my head. I jumped up and gave him a big hug. His coat smelled like campfire smoke.

Mrs. Lewis' beady eyes watched us over the top of her reading glasses. Naturally suspicious, she patted some wild hairs escaping the fat bun she always wore and tried to hear what we were saying.

Ordinarily nothing threw her, but I could understand how Grandfather did. A ten-gallon hat sat cocked on his forehead, and his coat, a smudged sheepskin duster, came down past his knees. He'd tucked his blue jeans into a pair of scuffed cowboy boots. Thick, white hair fell loose over his shoulders and halfway down his back. You see a lot of different people in New York, but none of them look quite like my grandfather. Not even close.

Mrs. Lewis recovered. She puckered her mouth like she was eating cranberries. "May I help you . . . um, sir?"

Grandfather tugged the brim of his hat and smiled. Almost like she couldn't help it, Mrs. Lewis smiled back. I was stunned. Usually she's a regular iceberg.

"I called earlier," said Grandfather. "I'm here to pick up my granddaughter. Her brother's not doing well. He's pretty sick, I'm afraid. She needs to see him. You're kind to release her on such short notice."

Mrs. Lewis raised her eyebrows. "Oh!" She shot me her best "tell me what you know or you'll be tortured" look.

"Miss Anderson, is this . . . um . . . gentleman your grandfather?"

I threw my backpack over my shoulder and nodded. "Yes, ma'am. This gentleman really is."

She bypassed the wisecrack. She was too busy studying Grandfather. Once she even tilted her head sideways like a dog does when it hears a funny noise. Then she said, "Just a moment please, I'll have to call your mother's office to make sure about this." As we waited she ruffled through some index cards and then checked out something on her computer screen.

"Oh? Mrs. Anderson's gone for the day? Very well, thank you." Mrs. Lewis hung up the phone and looked again at her computer. "Well, it says here that in the event that Mrs. Anderson is unavailable, you are the child's guardian. May I see some identification please?"

Grandfather took out his wallet and showed her his driver's license, which had his photograph on it.

"Hmmph . . ." she coughed. "Very well. So, all right, you may take the child with you."

I tugged Grandfather's sleeve and gave a big, fake cough myself. I was ready to go. I'd do anything to get out of my stupid third period French class. They always make you read aloud in front of the class. In French, of course. That about kills me.

Grandfather took the hint. As we turned to leave, Mrs. Lewis scuttled from behind her desk like a sand crab and blocked our path. She stuck a clipboard in Grandfather's face. "Sign this, please." Grandfather signed his name and sighed. "This is worse than renting a car." After he was through, he politely tipped his hat. Mrs. Lewis frowned and went back to her perch behind the desk.

We went out the door and down the front steps. It was a little after 9:00 a.m. I could just picture Emily squirming back in math class, dying to know what was happening.

A mix of snow and stinging sleet burned our faces. Above us, the sky was low and gray, the color of mop bucket water. I was absolutely bursting to ask Grandfather about Peter, but I knew he was of the Lakota belief that young people should be respectful, listening to their elders first and asking questions later. I felt sure he'd tell me about Peter when the time was right. We walked with our heads down. I held Grandfather's hand, the back of which was brown and crinkly as a walnut shell and just as rough. I was glad he'd rescued me. What I didn't know was why. Why did he come to me instead of Mom? And why did he take a red-eye back to New York before my brother was even hospitalized?

Something else was going on. I could feel it. Something strange. Let's face it; it was pretty weird how he just appeared. Still I kept my mouth shut. I figured he had a good reason for whatever he was doing. Mysterious but good. We walked to the next corner. As we waited for the light to change, he nudged me. "Did you eat breakfast?"

His question caught me off guard. I wrinkled my nose. "Uh huh, I had a bagel and half an orange."

"Good."

"Why?"

"We've got a lot of work to do."

I thought about that one for a second. The light changed. As we stepped into the crosswalk, I tried the indirect approach. "Did *you* eat breakfast?"

Grandfather squeezed my hand. "I bought a blueberry muffin from a pastry cart in the airport concourse, but I didn't eat it. I just had a cup of coffee."

I smiled. Grandfather loves coffee . . . as long as it's bad. He likes it strong and as thick as molasses. He always teases me and says it's no good unless a teaspoon can stand up in it.

He patted his pocket. "You want the muffin?"

I laughed. "No, thanks." We walked a few more steps. I was freezing and Grandfather wasn't talking. Trained in Lakota ways or not, the suspense was killing me. Finally I had to come right out and ask. "Grandfather, please tell me what's wrong with Peter. Is it the fever again? Has it gotten worse?"

He pursed his lips and nodded. "Yes, the fever. It's serious this time. Your mother is at the hospital. She called your father, and he's flying into La Guardia this afternoon."

The fever. Exactly what I figured. I hate to admit it, but for a tiny second I was mad. To tell the truth I was sick of Peter and his stupid fever and how preoccupied it made Mom. I mean, I know how selfish it sounds, but I was tired of him always being sick and getting attention. About the only time Mom paid any attention to me lately was to yell at me for messing up something, like getting a bad grade in math or leaving dirty dishes in the sink. And we'd always gotten along so well. Now it seemed like absolutely everything I did was wrong. It made things around the house really depressing. And it's not like Mom had exactly been a big ball of fun since the divorce anyway.

Just then we passed the doorway of an abandoned storefront. From the shadows inside a weak voice called: "Change? Spare change?"

Grandfather immediately went over. I rolled my eyes. He constantly does stuff like this. It takes us practically forever to get out of the subway sometimes because he's always giving money to the people who ask. And he's not rich!

The doorway smelled like a public restroom at Coney Island in August. There were broken wine bottles and trash everywhere. I couldn't see much more than a pair of bloodshot eyes staring out between a dirty knit cap and the top of a ragged blanket. The poor guy was trembling so hard he was almost a blur. Grandfather put his hand on his shoulder and leaned close in his face to listen. After they talked a little bit, he gave the man the muffin from his pocket and a five-dollar bill. We started down the sidewalk again.

"That was nice," I said.

Grandfather grunted. "We're all one family. Always remember that."

We walked some more. The pavement was packed with people hurrying along without looking at you in the way they always do in New York. We were on Central Park West. It was getting colder, but luckily our apartment wasn't far.

Grandfather's surprise appearance kept bothering me. Was Peter dying? Why didn't Grandfather tell me anything?

Was he trying to keep me from panicking? Adults always do stuff like that. Respect for my elders or not, while we were waiting to cross another side street, I finally asked him point-blank: "You sure got here fast. When . . . uh . . . when did you say Mom called you this morning?"

Before he answered, the "WALK" sign came on. We stepped into the street, pushed along like bumper cars by the crowd behind us. "Actually she didn't call me. I found out last night," he shouted over the noise of a passing bus.

I stopped dead in the middle of the crosswalk. A cabbie rolled down his window and yelled at us. A snowflake landed on my nose. I rubbed it away. "Last night? Peter was home with me last night watching television. He was fine. How did you know he was going to . . . you know . . . be sick?"

A strange light came into his eyes. "A ghost told me."

CHAPTER THREE

*T*he traffic light changed. I didn't move. The swollen-faced taxi driver angrily punched his horn. I waved for him to go around. He swerved past us, only taking the phone out of his ear long enough to mouth some choice words. As he roared away, he smashed into a monster pothole and sprayed gray slush all over my new snow boots.

I wiggled my little finger in my ear. "What did you say? I thought you said *ghost*!" I put my hands on my hips and faced Grandfather.

"Come over to the curb before you get us both killed," answered Grandfather. "Our friends are losing patience." He jerked a thumb toward the river of yellow taxis jammed up behind us.

We regrouped on the far corner next to a phone kiosk. I didn't even know those things still existed in New York. I'd only seen them in movies. Doesn't everybody carry a cell phone now? Two of the three phones looked like giant wolverines or something had chewed them. A short fellow who looked to be wearing every stitch of clothing he owned was on the third phone, yelling at someone named Gloria.

"A ghost?" I shouted.

The phone guy stopped yelling and looked nervously at Grandfather and me. Then he turned his back and resumed griping at poor old Gloria.

"A ghost?" I asked again, this time lowering my voice and raising my eyebrows.

Grandfather nodded. "Yes, my grandmother. Her spirit visits me every once in awhile. Usually she has important news, although sometimes she just drops in to check on me and see how I'm doing."

He said this as casually as I would tell someone about brushing my teeth.

I suddenly realized I didn't know him as well as I thought I did. It was a weird feeling, but I liked it. I really love mysteries, like I really love my Grandfather. "You're joking, right?"

"Our ancestors are always with us, Granddaughter. They live in our hearts. In our waking and sleeping, and especially in our hours of need, they're with us. The Lakota people, your people, have always known this."

"Well, I mean, what . . . how . . . where do you see her?"

"Lots of places. Sometimes in the park. One time in the lobby at Radio City Music Hall. She likes the apartment, too."

The idea of my long-dead Lakota great-grandmother cruising around our apartment was a little hard to take. "Where did you see her this time?" I asked, still in shock.

"In the sweat lodge. My nephew Russell Strong Bird and I built one down by the creek on the reservation. We were conducting an *inipi*."

"A what?"

"An *inipi*. It's a rite of purification that gets us closer to the Creator." I knew I must still have looked confused because my grandfather continued to explain. "First, we use willow saplings to make a frame about the size of an upside-down rowboat. Then we cover that in buffalo hides. Inside this we dig a fire pit. Next, we build a fire and heat up some rocks. When the rocks are hot, we crawl inside the lodge and pour water on them. The rocks turn bright red and hiss like rattlesnakes. The steam billows like fog and hurts your eyes."

"What do you wear? A bathing suit or something?"

"Nope, we enter the lodge in the same outfit that we entered the world."

The picture of my nude grandfather flashed through my mind. It was a little unsettling. "Is it, like, a health thing?" We talked like this a lot, my Grandfather and I, always going off on tangents, as my mother would say while rolling her eyes impatiently. And I never minded when he'd leave the subject and just pick up and go off on one.

He laughed. "Nope, as I said, it's a purification ceremony. We pray and try to get right with the Creator and Mother Earth. We try to get purified so that we can live as they want us to. Sometimes, if we get really pure, we see visions."

"And you saw your grandmother?"

"Her face appeared in the smoke. She said Peter was really sick and I had to save him. Then she vanished. Well, I can tell you I came out of that lodge pretty fast. It was a beautiful, clear night. Cold but beautiful. When I lifted my arms to pray, I saw a shooting star. It was like a Roman candle on the Fourth of July. I knew it was time to go. I made Russell drive me in his pickup straight to the nearest airport as soon as we got dressed. I took the earliest flight they had."

I knew he was telling the truth, or at least what he thought was the truth. I'd never known him to do anything else. "How are you going to save Peter?"

He looked down the street. A garbage truck rumbled past, belching exhaust. In the distance, a police siren wailed. "Traditionally some sort of healing ceremony would be in order. In fact I already have a plan in mind. And I need your help if it's going to work," he announced, staring straight into my eyes.

I felt a little shiver of excitement. This was it, of course. "Is that why you got me out of school?"

"Yes. I didn't think you'd mind skipping."

He sure as heck was right about that. I scratched my head. "Well, when did . . . um . . . when did you really, really find out Peter was sick?" As soon as the words were out of my mouth, I realized I sounded like I didn't believe in his vision. So I corrected myself: "I mean, when did Mom speak to you? How did she know you were home?"

"I called her office first thing when I got to the apartment. She'd just gotten off the phone with the school. Peter collapsed right after he got there. She was on her way to the emergency room to meet the ambulance." He bit his lip and looked at the pavement.

"Poor Peter," I sighed. The situation sounded pretty grim. I suddenly felt guilty over being angry with him earlier. I pictured my brother falling down in front of his classmates. And you know kids; I bet some of them laughed. And now he was in the hospital, where he had to be scared and confused. Poor little guy, to think I was angry with him. But I forced myself to put these thoughts and feelings aside. What could I do about it? It happened, and I wasn't there to help him when it did. My eyes began to tear up. I shook my head. Instinctively I knew that I had to stay strong. This was no time to go to pieces. So I changed the subject. "Didn't Mom think it was weird that you were back? I mean, you weren't supposed to be home until the weekend."

He squinted at me. "I told her I was bored and came home early. She had other things on her mind anyway. I asked to go to the hospital, too, but she said I'd only be in the way, that I should wait at home." He gave a sad sort of laugh. "I guess she doesn't need an old man to take care of, too."

I could tell that Mom had hurt his feelings. Not that he'd ever say anything to her about it. It's not his style to complain. I wondered if she'd told him to keep me out of the way, too. Probably.

A heavy snow began to fall. Big, moist flakes fluttered around us like confetti as our breaths steamed the air. We obviously couldn't save Peter if we froze to death on a street corner. I made a suggestion. "Why don't we head home for some hot cocoa before we begin our mission?"

"No, we need to keep moving. Peter is depending on us."

I tightened the straps on my backpack. "Are we going straight to the hospital?"

Grandfather looked around. "Later." He pointed to a nearby shoe store. "Let's go inside for a minute where it's warm. It's time you knew."

'Knew what?' I wondered. Still I dared not ask yet. Grandfather would tell me when the time was right. It was useless to force him to say something. I could only get away with that once in a while, but not this time, which I knew as surely as I was standing there.

Once we were inside, a clerk approached us. When he got a good look at Grandfather, he pulled up short like he wasn't too sure he wanted to come any closer. Coughing nervously, he asked, "May I—may I help you?"

"No, thanks," Grandfather answered firmly, "we're just browsing."

The poor clerk looked relieved. He adjusted the red carnation in his lapel and went to help another customer with some tacky stiletto pumps.

Grandfather motioned to a nearby chair. "Take a seat. I have to tell you something." Unsure of what to expect, I sat down. Grandfather sat next to me. My heart beat against my ribs. Here it was.

"Feather, our little one is . . ." He stared deep into my eyes. ". . . he's not doing well."

I nodded. Grandfather bit his lip and thought a minute.

"In the old days," he said slowly, "when one of the helpless ones was ill, the Lakota people would ask Mother Earth for a healing. To show how deeply they cared and to prove they were worthy of this healing, the People went on vision quests. They'd go to a lonely mountaintop and cry for a vision. They'd have adventures, you might say, amongst the animals, the trees and the hills. Amongst all Mother Earth's children. It was very *wakan*, very mysterious and holy."

He paused, as if listening to faraway music. "I'm old now, but my spirit is still strong." He patted his chest. "We must help Peter, you and I. I've been watching you closely over the years, Feather. As you've grown into a young woman, I've seen that you possess the 'gift'."

"The gift?"

"The gift of healing. If you're willing, I can teach you the old ways. This gift is a powerful one. I can guide you to use it wisely."

He watched my face for a reaction. "Will you go on this quest with me? Will you walk this path of the heart with me to save Peter?"

—

I didn't need to think. "You know I'll go anywhere with you, Grandfather."

He bit his lip, like he was fighting not to cry. And then he bent down and hugged me close to him.

I took his hand and we went out into the snow.

CHAPTER FOUR

"Where are we going first, Grandfather?"

"FAO Schwarz."

This wasn't exactly the answer I expected. FAO Schwarz isn't a very mysterious place. Fun, but not mysterious.

"The toy store?"

Grandfather chuckled. "Yes, to start I'd like to get Peter a present. After that, well, after that, we'll see."

The weather was getting worse. Snow clouds swirled in the streets like runaway gangs of ballerinas gone wild. I pulled my scarf up over my nose. The sky was low and ugly. The tops of the taller office towers were chopped off and shrouded in fog. A fierce wind howled angrily between the buildings, making the traffic lights over the intersections bob like they were made of rubber. Steam gushed from the sewers. I was glad I had on my heaviest coat.

We walked a couple of blocks with our heads bent against the wind. The sidewalks were slick as grease, and dirty snow was piled up in the gutters at every corner. Twice, people in front of us slipped. Thankfully Grandfather hailed a cab. As soon as his arm went up, a cab magically appeared out of the blizzard and pulled up to the curb.

"Let's ride awhile," Grandfather said. He opened the rear door. He didn't look cold. I knew he was more worried about me. I started to climb inside the taxi, but he put his hand on my arm and stopped me.

"Listen," he whispered, his head turning slightly upward.

The wind howled. "Wh-What?" I asked. My teeth chattered.

Grandfather pointed to the sky. "To our brother, Sunka Manitou, the Wolf. He's hunting with us. He gives help to those who know how to ask."

Suddenly the wind gusted and an icy burst of snow stung my cheeks. As I blinked, a blurry white shape raced by in the street. At least it seemed like it did. When I opened my eyes, it was gone. I couldn't tell what it was for sure, but it looked like a dog. A dog . . . or maybe a wolf? But that couldn't be. Could it? No way, I thought. I got in the cab.

It was warm in the backseat and clean, too, even the floorboard. That was a first. The entire cab smelled good, sort of like fresh-cut grass. It was a familiar smell. But from where? I tried to remember.

Grandfather slammed the door and spoke to the driver. "How, kola."

I knew what "How, kola" meant. It meant "Hello, friend." I wondered why Grandfather was speaking Lakota. When I looked at the driver, I nearly fainted.

He was one of the People! I couldn't see his face but his long, black hair was tightly braided. A delicately woven dream catcher trimmed with feathers and turquoise nuggets dangled from the rearview mirror.

Grandfather quietly talked to the cabbie as we rode through a snow-blanketed Central Park. I didn't understand anything except the words "FAO Schwarz." When we pulled up in front of the famous Fifth Avenue toy store's plate glass doors only a few minutes later, I felt a terrific rush of excitement. And I forgot about Peter! To tell the truth, I forgot about everything. I couldn't wait to get in the store. What a surprise to suddenly be there in the middle of a school day!

Located on Fifth Avenue, right across from the famous Plaza Hotel, where the "Eloise" story was set, FAO Schwarz is like the best place in the whole world . . . to me, at least, and I bet to nearly every other kid in New York. It's like the most famous toy shop ever. Two floors of fun, it's got this huge doll section featuring a life-size Barbie in a tiara and a pink ball gown, a Muppet shop, a pottery studio, any kind of arts and crafts supplies you could want, eco-friendly toys, bikes and scooters of every description, more board games than you can imagine and a giant piano keyboard on the floor that plays music and lights up when you dance on it. Very best of all, it has this humongous stuffed animal section. That's my number one stop. Some of my happiest memories are of when Dad would be in town on one of his rare visits after Mom and he got divorced and he'd take Peter and me there. He'd feel so guilty about not seeing us much that he'd let us buy anything we wanted . . . and we would! As soon as we set foot in the door, Peter and I would run in different directions, heading to our favorite sections, me to the plush toys and Peter to the Transformers and Legos. It was like a dream come true—every time.

Grandfather paid the driver while I tightened one of my boots. When I stood up, the taxi had mysteriously vanished. I looked down the street, but I couldn't see it anywhere. A spooky feeling came over me. I shivered . . . and this time not with the cold.

Grandfather put his arm around my shoulders. "Cold, Takoja?"

I rubbed my elbows. "Yeah, brrr."

Grandfather held the door open for me. "Let's go find Peter a toy. Something that will make him feel strong," he said. Then, like he'd read my mind, he added, "Oh, he was one of the Blue Cloud People from Montana, an Arapaho, as the whites call them. It felt good to talk the old talk with him."

I looked at Grandfather. "Isn't it kind of, I don't know, weird, that his cab was the first one to come by? I mean, out of all the cabs in the city?"

Grandfather's eyes twinkled. "These things happen, Feather. These things happen. You'll understand more when you're ready."

The place was packed. Bigger kids yelled and ran everywhere and swarms of snow-suited toddlers were getting dragged along by red-faced parents. Grandfather chuckled and took in the happy scene. "What do you suggest we get your brother?"

I didn't even have to think about it. "A fire engine! He always goes bananas when he sees one on the street or when he hears sirens from our apartment."

We made our way to the second floor, next to the rollerblades and skateboards, and there we found a bright, red fire engine that had a working siren, flashing lights and a retractable ladder. It was perfect! Peter would go crazy for it. Mom would go crazy for it, too, but in a different way. The siren was pretty annoying.

Grandfather paid in cash and asked the salesperson to wrap it. While we waited for her, he asked me if there was anything I wanted.

It was really hard to say "No," but I had to. I knew he didn't have much money.

But he wouldn't take no for an answer. "Listen. Maybe there's a small thing that calls out to you. This is a special day, you know. We should honor it. What speaks to your heart?"

"Well, stuffed animals are my very favorite, you know," I said. I mean I could only be so good.

"I hear them calling, too," Grandfather smiled. "You're wise to listen to the four-leggeds. They are our teachers. They've been here on Mother Earth longer than we have. They know a lot." I loved when Grandfather talked this way about our "four-legged brothers and sisters and our winged, finned, and clawed cousins." He always called them our family and our teachers.

Grandfather thanked the clerk and tucked the package under his arm like a football. "Let's go then and visit the animals," he winked at me.

We rode the escalator to the first floor where the stuffed animal pavilion occupied a whole corner of the store. Shelves bulged with everything from fuzzy mice to almost life-sized gorillas and lions.

I spotted a beautiful baby snow leopard. I thought of my collection of endangered species on my bed at home. I already had a rhino, a tiger, a blue whale, and a panda. Dad always gave them to me on special occasions. I didn't have a leopard, though. I reached for it.

"Wait," Grandfather said. "Listen." He tapped his heart.

I wasn't exactly sure what he meant, so I just stood really still. Suddenly a sparkling, coal-black eye peeked out from beneath a pile of teddy bears. I stuck my hand in the furry pile and out came a white buffalo. She was so cute! She had stubby nubbins of horns, a black button nose, and a soft, white coat. I fell in love with her on the spot.

"May I have her, Grandfather?"

"You don't have a choice. You already belong to her. The Old Ones called her White Buffalo Calf Girl. Later I'll tell you a story about her."

After everything else that had happened, I was suspicious of a set-up. "Did you know she was there, Grandfather?"

"No. But you did. That's what's important," he said.

I didn't know what to think. Strange things kept happening, from the ghostly wolf to the Native American cab driver, and now the buffalo. I wished I could call my friend Emily, but she was in school.

We paid for my buffalo. I wanted to hold her, so I told the clerk I didn't need a bag. "I'm ready for the next part of our adventure, Tunkashila." I looked up at him happily, taking his big hand in mine.

"Good," he replied. "Let's go!"

Outside, the snow was really coming down. We headed toward the Plaza Hotel. With all the snow, it looked like a gigantic, fairytale wedding cake. It's a very fancy place. I've never been inside, but I've seen what it looks like in the movies and books. Someday I'm going to stay there in a huge suite and order chocolate sundaes from room service!

Grandfather didn't even glance up. I wondered if he knew what a ritzy place it was. Probably not. He doesn't much care about fancy stuff. I guess that's better than worrying about it all the time, like lots of people do.

"Mind if we go to the park for a minute?" he asked. "I want to tell you that story."

"I'm game." I clutched my buffalo under my chin. She was warm.

We stopped on the edge of Central Park. The snow was two feet deep. The trees, all naked and spindly, looked like they were frosted with powdered sugar. Some little kids squealed and hollered in the distance as they sledded down a hill. Their happy noise made me feel good.

Grandfather pointed to a clump of bare oak trees. His breath came out in puffs of steam. "Look, Feather. Close your eyes and look with your heart. Often, what you see with your eyes shut is what counts the most."

I squinted toward the trees. "What, Grandfather? What do you want me to see?"

"I want you to imagine the lodges of the People gathered in a circle. See the smoke rising from the tipis; hear the low voices of the elders murmuring inside as they tell stories around the campfire. If you listen closely enough, you'll hear the children laughing."

I looked and listened. From far away, I did hear children's laughter. And if I closed my eyes just enough, I could see the people's lodges tall against the snow. Almost.

"Not long ago, the People roamed across Mother Earth, following the great nation of Tatanka, the sacred buffalo. We stepped lightly on our mother, careful to leave nothing behind but our prayers. When Old Man

Winter came, beating his drum and singing his medicine songs of wind and ice, we gathered in our lodges in a circle amongst the trees and told stories to pass the long, dark days—days poor in food but rich in love and stories. One story we told was the legend of White Buffalo Calf Girl."

"Like my buffalo, Grandfather?"

Grandfather smiled. "Yes, Feather, like your buffalo. The most important story the People told was about her."

"Really?"

"It's true. When I was a little boy, I myself heard the story of my own grandfather. Just as I recall him telling it before the fire while the embers popped and cracked, it goes like this: Long ago, in the time of the ancient ones, two young Lakota hunters, not much older than you, searched for food on a winter's day, a cold day, much like this one. They were hunting to feed the helpless ones. In the old days, nothing was held more honorable than to help those who couldn't help themselves."

I thought about a homeless woman we saw earlier in the morning huddled inside a cardboard box on top of a steam grate. "It's not like that any more, is it?"

Grandfather sadly shook his head. "No. Many people have forgotten the old ways. The circle of life is broken."

I felt bad for interrupting. "I'm sorry, Grandfather. Go on. What did the hunters find?"

"As they stood on a hill, searching for game, they spotted something in the distance coming toward them. Like a mirage, it mysteriously flickered and floated above the ground, going in and out of focus like a picture in a dream. And then they saw. It was a beautiful young woman, dressed in a white deerskin dress and bearing a pack on her shoulders. The hunters couldn't believe their eyes. They thought that maybe they were seeing things because they were so hungry. Their stomachs growled and pinched against their ribs. They rubbed their eyes. But, no, the beautiful young woman came closer. Soon they knew she was *waken*— mysterious and sacred."

"What did the woman do, Grandfather? Did she tell them where to find food?"

"She did something more important than food, Takoja. She told them where to find Meaning in Life."

"Meaning in Life?" I wrinkled my nose.

"The mysterious woman accompanied the hunters to their village. All the people gathered in the great council lodge to see this beautiful and wonderful stranger. Before all the people, she opened her pack and gave them many sacred things. These objects are still treasured and hidden away by our people on our sacred lands. The Lakota nation's sacred pipe is one of them. She also gave the people a message."

"What message, Grandfather?"

"She said that the Planet Earth is our Mother, and that she is holy. Every stride we take across her body should be pure and sincere, like a fountain of love flowing from our hearts. Most of all, she said the people must always remember that the two-leggeds, the four-leggeds, and all other creatures who live on, above, and below this Earth are sacred, too, and should be treated as such, for they are our brothers and sisters. Then the mysterious woman left the lodge."

"She just left?"

"Yes," Grandfather said gently. "As you can imagine, all the people, all the men, women, and boys and girls, ran pleading after the beautiful and mysterious woman, begging for her to stay and live with them always. The little ones tugged on the fringed hem of her dress. Gently, but firmly, she refused. She said it could not be. And then, as all the people watched, she floated away over the snow-covered prairie, and, just as she reached the top of a faraway ridge, she transformed herself into a white buffalo and vanished like a patch of morning fog that suddenly burns away before the sun."

I had a hard time swallowing this last part. "Do . . . do you think the story is true?"

"Well, I believe what the woman said is true, yes."

Using the back of my mitten I wiped my nose, which was starting to drip. I tried to sneak it, but Grandfather noticed. I immediately got mad at myself. I didn't want him worrying about me.

"Today we are like those two young braves, Granddaughter. We've met White Buffalo Calf Girl," said Grandfather.

"We have, haven't we?" I patted her.

"And now," he said, "our quest continues. For this part of our journey, we'll take the subway. Are you ready?"

"I'm ready," I replied eagerly, as I knocked the snow off my shoulders.

Grandfather pulled my wool cap further down over my ears. "How about a hot pretzel, first? With lots of mustard." He motioned to a steaming pretzel stand drawing a big crowd on the nearest corner.

"Sounds good to me!" I exclaimed. Suddenly I was starving. As we crossed the street, I could still hear the children laughing in the park.

CHAPTER FIVE

While Grandfather went to the machine and bought our fares for the subway, I finished my pretzel. After I brushed the salt and crumbs off White Buffalo Calf Girl, I joined him at the turnstile and as we pushed through together, I asked, "Where are we going now, Grandfather?"

"To Greenwich Village. My old friend Mrs. Chen has a special order waiting for me at her store."

I hadn't been to the Village in ages. The last time was to go shopping with Mom. She loves all the little boutiques and art galleries there. It's a very cool place. I wasn't familiar with Mrs. Chen's store, though. It was almost lunchtime and the platform was packed. I stood close to Grandfather.

Soon the grimy, silver train arrived with its usual clatter and whoosh of air. After some shoving, we got on and found a seat. The doors screeched shut and the cars jerked. Most of the passengers stared at the floor or hung on the straps, gazing blankly into space like they were trying to shut themselves off from everyone around them. Nearly all of them looked either bored or sad. The only person who seemed content was a red-cheeked little kid busily sucking on a Tootsie Pop.

Grandfather's face reflected in the window. He didn't look bored or sad. I think he saw some of those things you see when your eyes are shut. You know, the things that count the most. In a moment, he unbuttoned his coat. He fished around and pulled out his most closely guarded possession—his deerskin medicine bundle. My eyes got big. I knew then that something special was going to happen before the day was over. And I knew in my heart it all had to do with saving Peter.

With his eyes still shut, he cradled the bundle in his arms and then whispered a prayer in Lakota. Inside the beaded deerskin bag were objects that meant something important to him: a smooth stone he found on top of a holy mountain; an eagle feather from his first vision quest; hawk feathers given to him by his great-grandfather; a piece of cloth from Grandmother's wedding dress. There were other things in the bag, too. Sacred things. Things I didn't know about. Not yet, anyway.

The train crawled into the next station. Grandfather buttoned the medicine bag back inside his coat, back where it was safe, and said, "One more stop and we'll be in the Village. Mrs. Chen is anxious to meet you."

This was news. "You told her I was coming? How could you be sure I'd be with you?" I asked in surprise.

"Let's just say I had a good feeling about it."

"Tell me about her, Grandfather. Who is Mrs. Chen? Have you guys been friends for very long? What's her store like?"

"You'll like her store, Takoja. And you will like her even more. She's wise and generous and funny. I met her years ago. We've been best friends ever since. It was a great day in my life when she moved to New York. Right now I'm sure she'll have lunch waiting for us, with lots of hot green tea."

Lunch? Grandfather must've arranged the whole day from start to finish. He was being pretty mysterious about it, too. I liked that.

"Yes, I've known Mrs. Chen for years. More than I can remember!" Grandfather chuckled. "She was born in Hong Kong. My ship dropped anchor there back in my merchant marine days, back when I still had the Great Sadness and was drinking." He paused and gazed out the window. "She saved my life."

"Wha—?" My question was stifled when the train lurched out of the station. I stroked White Buffalo Calf Girl. I knew about the Great Sadness. Many years ago, on the reservation, the Lakota children were taken from their parents and shipped like cattle to the white people's boarding schools. There the teachers cut off the children's long hair and punished them if they spoke their own language. It was terrible. Why didn't they want them to be Indians anymore? I could never under-stand that. One day they came for Grandfather when he was only seven. On his thirteenth birthday he escaped. He said the school was worse than prison. When he got home, he learned his mother was dead from a fever. The sadness almost killed him. Then he hitchhiked west until he reached the sea.

The graffiti-sprayed walls of the subway tunnel raced by. Grandfather shut his eyes again. I hated to bother him, but there was something I had to know. "You said that Mrs. Chen saved your life. What did you mean?"

"She did. Nearly sixty years ago. You know how I went to sea, right?"

"Yes."

"I wanted to get as far away from the reservation as I could. My heart hurt. I couldn't bear the pain of my mother's death and seeing what happened to the People. We'd lost everything . . . our land, our way of life, our stories, and our little ones. Our whole way of being, our sacred way, which was thousands of years old, was stolen. I thought the ocean would make me forget."

"Did it, Grandfather?"

"No . . . no, it didn't. So, like a fool, I drank. One day my ship, a leaky, rusted oil tanker barely able to float, berthed in Hong Kong. I went ashore, sniffing around for whiskey, like a dog." Grandfather's face crinkled. "I was in sad shape, believe me. As it grew dark, I stumbled into a smoky café, thinking it was a saloon. A nice young woman was wiping down tables."

"Mrs. Chen?"

"Yes, Takoja, it was she. And do you know what she said?"

I shook my head.

"She said, 'It's about time. I've been waiting for you'!"

"No way!"

"I admit . . . it's a funny sort of story. Still, it's true. Improbable things are often true. Sometimes the most improbable. Anyway, I staggered in and sat down. After she took one look at me, she knew my heart was in bad shape. She brought me a cup of hot tea."

"How did she know you were coming?"

"From a dream, my granddaughter. From a dream."

My mouth fell open. He smiled at my surprise.

"She dreamt that a young man in need was coming from across the sea. For many months, nothing happened. Still, she waited. When I walked in, she knew the young man in her dream was me. Sometimes our dreams are wiser than our waking thoughts."

The train pulled into our stop. People pushed down the aisle like it was a jailbreak. I didn't budge. "So how did she save your life?"

"She gave me back my story," Grandfather whispered with great feeling.

"I don't understand."

"She simply listened to me. In the warmth of her kindness, my heart opened like a sunflower. Over many cups of tea, I told her about my past. About my mother. About all the bad things done to our people and how our beautiful land was stolen from us. About how I hated the whites for their cruelty and lies."

I looked at all the grim faces crowding past us. "Do you still hate the whites?"

"No, Takoja. Hatred destroys the hater. Don't ever forget that. My own hatred almost drowned me in alcohol. Of course, what the whites did was wicked. I know that if I know anything on this earth, and I will never forget it. But I am no longer bitter. Bitterness poisons the heart. That I know, too," he said. He bowed his head and added, "I learned the hard way."

"But I still don't get it. How did Mrs. Chen give you back your story?"

"She told me to go home. She said running away from your problems only gives them power. She suggested I go back and help my people, and live out in my own life all the good things they stood for. I listened. I returned to the reservation and became a Lakota again. My roaming days were over. I settled down to my real full-time job—being myself."

"What did you do, Grandfather?"

"Well, for one thing, one very good thing. I met your grandmother. Later, she and I started a school. The old ways were disappearing and it made us sad. We decided it would be a good thing to teach the reservation children what we learned at our own grandparents' knees. We wanted to preserve their hard-won wisdom. Mainly we told the kids the ancient stories about our brothers and sisters . . . you know, the animals."

"Like the stories you told me when I was a little girl? About Coyote the Trickster, and how Rabbit stole fire from the Sky People?"

"The very same ones."

"What else did you do?"

"On warm days, we took them on hikes up in the sacred hills to find medicine plants. In the winter, we stayed inside by the fire, beading moccasins, making drums, and painting hides. In helping these little ones find themselves, I slowly rediscovered who I was, too. I found my story. Each person has one, you know. You are now on the path of yours."

The subway car groaned and jerked forward. I realized we'd missed our stop.

"Grandfather! Hurry! We need to get off!"

"Don't panic, dear one. You'll scare White Buffalo Calf Girl! Besides, we'll get off at the next opportunity. Mrs. Chen is patient. She'll wait." He was always so calm like that—about everything, it seemed.

And just like he said, we got off at the next station. When we got upstairs the storm was worse. Icy gusts of wind bit at our noses. As we trudged through deserted Washington Square, snow fell in buckets. It was hard to walk and harder to see. The square's famous arch was almost invisible and snow was so deep you couldn't tell where the sidewalk left off and the street began. I held Grandfather's hand real tight.

A lone taxi idled on the far side of the square. From the exhaust pipe, white smoke curled like a crouching dragon. The sign on top glowed. "Ah, we're rescued," said Grandfather warmly, sounding very pleased.

I thought he was teasing. To my surprise, the taxi pulled up and the driver cranked down the passenger window. "How about a lift, my friends? The snow clouds are too strong for you to be afoot."

I peered inside the taxi—straight into the eyes of the Native American cabbie. The hair on the back of my neck stood on end.

CHAPTER SIX

Grandfather nudged me. "Go on, hop in."

I stayed glued to the curb. Somehow it felt like my whole body was made out of mud. After Grandfather cued me a second time, I somehow managed to work my legs and fall into the backseat.

For the second time in only a few hours, we were riding in the mysterious cab. In all my eleven years of living in New York City I don't think I'd ever had the same cab driver twice. I wondered what the odds were on getting one twice in the same day, in opposite parts of town, no less. This was a real coincidence. Or was it?

"Mrs. Chen's, please," Grandfather ordered, unfazed.

The driver silently nodded and merged into the ghostly fleet of cars navigating the icy streets. Outside the window snowflakes swirled before my eyes. The whole day was beginning to feel like a dream. After a minute, I snapped out of it and tugged Grandfather's sleeve. "Does he know Mrs. Chen, too?" I whispered.

Grandfather laughed. "Yes, angel. Many of the People do. She's an old friend to us."

Four long blocks later, the cab stopped in front of a crumbling brownstone storefront. Like most of the other addresses in this rundown section of the Village, its windows were boarded with plywood. "Chen's Imports Ltd." was painted over the door in faded letters. The place looked deserted. From the sidewalk, I watched the cab until it drove away. Instead of vanishing, it simply eased down the street; its red taillights winking like the eyes of a cat. After expecting something odd to happen, I was sort of disappointed.

That feeling didn't last long. When Grandfather raised his hand to knock on Mrs. Chen's door, something spooky really did happen. The door creaked open by itself. "Ah, she's expecting us," said Grandfather. He stepped aside so I could go first.

I shook my head. "No, thanks. You go ahead."

Grandfather stepped into the darkened doorway.

Afraid of what I might see, I peeked around him. My eyes grew real big because I couldn't believe what I saw.

As plain as the outside of Mrs. Chen's storefront looked, the inside was . . . whatever the opposite of plain is. Sparkling! Like the whole place was a treasure chest. I'd never seen so much stuff in my life! Fantastic, amazing, unbelievable stuff! In a way it reminded me of Aladdin's cave. The entire store was lit by a bunch of stubby scented candles and paper lanterns. It was the most colorful sight I'd ever seen—all kinds of statues and jewelry and paintings and wall hangings. Flocks of Chinese dragon kites hung from the ceiling, and, in the flickering candlelight, the dragons' eyes followed you. And that was just for starters.

"Wow!" I muttered.

I stepped inside. African dance masks stared out from the wall among towering piles of merchandise that spilled over nearly every square inch of the floor. Gleaming rows of oriental vases lined the shelves, and dusty wooden crates labeled in foreign languages were stacked everywhere, along with reams of printed fabric and woven baskets. Dried flowers, spices, herbs, and red chili peppers hung from posts. Beaded necklaces, earrings, bangles, and bracelets spilled like raindrops over the counters. The whole store was a United Nations of shopping.

Nobody seemed to be around, so I picked up a Japanese teacup and traced over its delicate design with my thumb. That did it. As if on cue, suddenly someone pushed through the beads hanging in the doorway behind the cash register. I dropped the teacup and it shattered on the floor.

"Good," chirped a voice. "I'm not the only one who breaks things around here." A sweet, delicate laugh floated across the store. It was like the music of a child, free and fearless with a hint of mischief. I was out of danger and breathed a sigh of relief.

"Mrs. Chen, it's good to see you again!" Grandfather exclaimed as the tiniest, oldest person I'd ever seen appeared out of the shadows and hugged him.

My jaw dropped. Mrs. Chen looked like—I promise I'm not making this up—a troll doll. She was barely four feet tall, if that. She wore a short Chinese silk jacket with orange dragons embroidered all over it, blue jeans, and red Keds. Her face was wrinkled as a peach pit and encircled by a halo of white curls. Next to her, Grandfather looked like a baby. Her eyes weren't old though. Even in the candlelight, they sparkled like emeralds.

"Mrs. Chen, I'd like you to meet Feather," said Grandfather proudly, turning to me.

The old lady held up a hand not much bigger than a doll's. There was a ring on every finger. A plump, jade dragon coiled around her pinky.

"This is a happy day, indeed! I am so pleased to meet you, Feather."

"Hi, um, nice to meet you, too." Not quite sure what to do, I hesitated a little and then shook her hand. Her grip was strong.

"Are you ready for lunch? Of course you are. Come into my kitchen where it's warm."

"Yes, Mrs. Chen, we're hungry," replied Grandfather with enthusiasm.

Mrs. Chen winked at me. "Splendid, come along." She disappeared behind the waterfall of cheap plastic beads. Grandfather and I followed her. This time I went first.

On the other side of the beads was her apartment. For the most part, it looked like the store. Fantastically cluttered. I didn't get to see much because she quickly slipped through yet more beads. Then we were in her kitchen. I noticed an expensive cappuccino machine.

Mrs. Chen pointed to a rickety bamboo table. "Sit down," she ordered. We sat instantly. "Now, how about some herbal tea? It'll help your appetites."

"That sounds excellent," Grandfather answered. "But may I first use your phone? I need to call the hospital and check on my grandson."

Peter! I had almost forgotten about him in the midst of Mrs. Chen's strange, new world. Grandfather was right, of course. Peter came first.

Mrs. Chen fiddled with a kettle on the stove. "You

know where the phone is, Spotted Eagle. Go, give Peter my love . . . and take your time. Feather and I need to have a little talk."

After Grandfather vanished through yet another doorway, Mrs. Chen and I were alone. I was nervous. I wondered what she wanted to talk about. I started playing with the bow on Peter's present. "Remember your manners," said Mrs. Chen. "We have company."

"Excuse me?"

She didn't hear me. I suddenly realized she wasn't speaking to me. Apparently, she was having a conversation with the tea kettle. I wondered if she was crazy. She shook her finger at it, grumbled, and then lit the antique gas burner with a long kitchen match. After she blew out the match, she sat down next to me. "One has to be firm with tea kettles. They are lazy creatures by nature," she chirped. "Good-natured, but lazy."

She gave me a big smile. I felt a whole lot better. She reminded me of a Keebler elf. Then she patted my hand. "I've been waiting for this for a long time. Your tunkashila has told me all about you. And now I see you in the flesh in my kitchen. This is a good day."

At first, I couldn't say anything. To tell the truth, I was kind of amazed she knew the Lakota word for grandfather. But then I remembered about her being a good friend of the People. "He has? I mean . . . he's told you about me?" I blushed.

Her eyes twinkled. "Oh, he's told me everything."

I wondered what everything was. "He has?"

"He loves you very much, you know."

I stroked White Buffalo Calf Girl. I wondered what she was getting at.

"He says you are a very powerful person. That you have a good soul. That you are a medicine woman . . . or will be one day."

A medicine woman? My heart fluttered in my chest like a trapped bird.

Mrs. Chen patted my hand again. Her touch was warm, like an electric blanket. "Don't be scared, my child. I am a harmless great-grandmother. I only say what I know to be true."

I knew there was more. I waited for what she would say next.

It was her turn to look away. She stared off into the distance. "The truth is the last thing the world wants to hear. Yes, it's the hardest thing to hear . . . and the easiest thing to say . . . if you are willing to pay a price." She laughed and the room came alive with the sound of it. Then her dark eyes pinned me in my chair. "Feather?"

"Yes, ma'am?"

"Your grandfather is a mighty Wicasa Wakan. Do you know what that means?"

Wicasa Wakan? My face went blank. I knew they were Lakota words, but that was all.

"He is a holy man. A healer. The People come from all over Turtle Island to see him."

"Turtle Island?"

"You aren't familiar with the term?"

I shook my head.

"To your ancestors, Feather, the earth was thought to be a giant turtle floating in the middle of a vast sea. Unhurried and wise, the turtle is the symbol of Mother Earth and eternal life. Some Indians call America 'Turtle Island.' The ancient ones in California said when the turtle yawned, the mountains shook. Earthquakes, you know." She giggled.

I thought about what she said about Grandfather. I knew many Lakota people came to see him, some of them from as far away as Wyoming. I always thought they were just old friends from the reservation. "You mean Grandfather is like a doctor or something?"

"One of the best. You're like him, you know. He sees that. More than anything on Mother Earth, he wants you to learn the old ways. He wants to pass on the wisdom of the People to you. Before it's too late."

My lower lip twitched. "T-T-Too late?" Now she was scaring me.

"He needs you, Feather."

"But why?"

Mrs. Chen smiled. "Like me, he is no longer young. He won't be around forever. A long time still, yes, but not forever. Only Mother Earth lasts forever. He doesn't want what he knows to vanish with him. Therefore, he has chosen you to save the traditional ways of your people from extinction."

"Me?" I was flabbergasted. How can this be? I thought. I'm just a kid. "But why me?" I asked, completely confused.

Then Mrs. Chen motioned for me to come closer. Curious, I leaned toward her, wondering what she was going to say next. She got in my face and whispered, "Because, my child, you are special."

"S-S-Special?" I gulped.

Mrs. Chen tapped her chest. "You listen. With your heart."

"What about Mom?" I protested. "Why doesn't Grandfather pick her? She's smart, and she's a lawyer and all that."

"Your mother is well-intentioned. Spotted Eagle tells me she does much to help the People in her own way.

In fact, he said she goes to court next month to help get some tribal land back. But she doesn't listen like you do."

"Why?"

"She thinks the old ways are only made-up stories. They aren't real to her. Computers and lawsuits are real to her. Not stories."

I had to agree. Come to think of it, Mom sometimes did make fun of Grandfather when he wasn't around.

Mrs. Chen held up a finger. "Stories are the most real things of all, Feather. Stories and dreams."

The tea kettle whistled. The old woman rose and shuffled to the stove. "Your mother doesn't get it. You do." She quickly poured three steaming cups of dark green tea.

Suddenly, I wasn't so scared anymore. It felt pretty good to be chosen.

Mrs. Chen passed me a cup and saucer. "Feather, has anything out of the ordinary ever happened to you?"

I wrinkled my nose. "Out of the ordinary? Like strange?"

"Odd may be a better word . . . so odd you might be tempted to call it magic."

I thought about the snow wolf, the Indian cabbie, how the door opened by itself, and how a spirit told Grandfather that Peter was sick. And sometimes . . .

well, sometimes my dreams did seem . . . I don't know
. . . not like dreams. Sort of real, I guess. "Yes, ma'am.
I suppose you could say some, um, odd things have
happened to me."

"Were these events helpful?"

I scrinched my eyebrows, puzzled. "How do you
mean?"

"Did they seem meaningful? Meaningful coinci-
dences, perhaps. Let me put it another way. Were they
clues?"

"I guess so," I replied hesitantly.

"Has anything like this happened recently?"

I paused a second. "Y-Yes."

She looked at me out of the corners of her eyes,
almost teasing. "Today, especially?" She caught the look
in my eyes as if she read my mind. "Good." Her eyes
narrowed. "So what happened today?"

I told her everything. She sipped her tea and listened
with her eyes shut. When I finished, she opened her
eyes and said, "Then it is so. You are chosen. The sacred
powers of the universe are helping you see this."

I didn't know what to say. I stroked White Buffalo
Calf Girl.

"Feather, when you are living in a sacred manner,
when you have found your story—"

Startled, I glanced up at her. That's the same thing she told Grandfather years ago.

She noticed my surprise. "Yes, when you are following your story, life helps you along. Things happen that cannot be explained. They are everyday magic. And they are good."

She poured herself more tea. "Be brave, Feather. Be brave and follow your path. Great things will happen. Things you can't imagine in your wildest dreams." The steam from the tea wreathed her face like smoke from a campfire. She gave me a big smile. "That's all I have to say."

The beads rattled and Grandfather walked in. He took off his hat and smoothed his hair with his palm. He looked worried. I realized the news about Peter wasn't good. He sighed and placed his medicine bag on the table. "The little one won't wake up. His fever is high and the doctor doesn't know what to do." He looked at Mrs. Chen.

With compassion in her eyes, she silently handed him a cup of tea. Then she took my hand. She could read the worry in my face.

Grandfather sat and drank the tea quickly. He looked older and more tired than I'd ever seen. Yet I knew somehow everything would be all right because of him. He always made me feel that way. I touched his hand. "Tunkashila, I'll help you. Tell me what to do."

He looked at me and then at Mrs. Chen. She nodded.

"She knows, Spotted Eagle. She knows and she is ready."

Grandfather bowed his head. When he looked up, silver tear tracks shone on his cheeks like the face paint worn by the Old Ones.

"Thank you, my granddaughter. I was dying of sadness, but now I live again."

I jumped up and hugged his neck.

Mrs. Chen put her arms around both of us. "Come, my friends. You have work to do. But first, you must eat. It's cold outside and you need your strength for what lies ahead."

I rubbed my hands together. I love Chinese food. "What are we having for lunch, Mrs. Chen? Spring rolls? Dim sum? Sweet and sour chicken and egg drop soup?"

She put her hands on her hips. "We're having pizza! Now come help me chop mushrooms!"

CHAPTER SEVEN

I felt stuffed. Three pieces of pizza is my normal limit. Today I ate four. I don't know what her secret is, but Mrs. Chen makes the best pie in town. I ought to know, too. I bet Emily and I have been to every pizza place in Manhattan. I waited for Grandfather and Mrs. Chen to get something in the back. Meanwhile I was dying to look around the store, but I didn't want to sneak around without permission.

Actually, I felt a little sleepy. All Mrs. Chen's talk about dreams, stories, and sacred powers seemed far away as I sat at the table. A single, naked light bulb hung from the ceiling. The kitchen sink dripped. Everything seemed so ordinary. I looked at my watch. School was almost out. Pretty soon I could call Emily. There was no way she would believe what I'd already done today. No possible way.

Voices came from somewhere deep in the apartment. They grew louder and Grandfather and Mrs.

Chen reappeared. An air of seriousness entered the room, too. And Grandfather carried something I'd only seen in books. Cradled in his arms, like a baby he wanted to protect, was a medicine pipe. Some people call them peace pipes, although that's really not the best description. Medicine pipes are the most treasured sacred objects the People own. That much I knew.

I'd heard from Grandfather that hidden away on the reservation, someplace where the whites would never ever find it, was the original pipe White Buffalo Calf Girl gave to the Lakota nation. As long as the pipe survives, he said, so will the People.

"G-Grandfather," I stuttered, "wh-wh-where did you get that?"

"It's mine, Takoja, as it was my father's, and his father's, and his father's before him. Someday, my child, it will be yours. Through this pipe, our family petitions the Creator, Wakan Tanka, and Mother Earth whenever we are in deepest need . . . and only then. It has never failed us."

"May I hold it?"

Grandfather nodded. "It's not a toy, so be careful. It's a great mystery. Think good thoughts in your heart and you may take it."

Mrs. Chen's face was as grave as Grandfather's was. From her expression, I knew this was serious stuff. I swallowed hard and thought about how much I wanted Peter to get well. My fingers trembled as I reached out.

Grandfather stretched out his arms to me and I gently took the pipe. Almost three feet long, it had a bowl of smooth, red stone. The wooden stem was wrapped in buckskin and trimmed with blue, yellow and green beads. Hanging from the stem were rawhide fringes and a fan made of eagle feathers. It was beautiful.

My hands tingled. The pipe felt alive. I carefully gave it back to Grandfather.

"Tell me about it, Tunkashila."

He held the pipe at my eye level. "Well, Takoja, the bowl is carved from a soft stone found only in one place in Minnesota. Its red color symbolizes the blood of the People."

He touched the beads. "The yellow, blue, and green, along with the red, stand for the colors of the four directions. The eagle feathers here—" he brushed the fan "—represent the Great Spirit. When the pipe is offered, its smoke carries our prayers to Wakan Tanka above, Mother Earth below, and the holy winds of the Four Directions. So we believe."

"Grandfather, I know this is a kind of nosey question, but where do you keep it? The pipe, I mean."

"Mrs. Chen has a safe. A big one. It's a good place.

The pipe stays there in its case, wrapped in a star quilt made by your grandmother."

Entrusting Mrs. Chen with its safekeeping spoke volumes. He really trusted her.

"How often do you use it?"

"Not often. The last time was when your cousin Roger Thunderhawk went to the Gulf War many years ago. I prayed with the pipe and Wakan Tanka brought him back safely. Now it's time once more." He slipped the pipe back into its buckskin case. "We're going to take it to the hospital," he announced solemnly.

So he was taking the pipe on the street. That seemed kind of desperate to me. What if we got mugged? I mean, it had to be really valuable. More than anything else, this clued me in to how worried Grandfather was. He obviously knew more about Peter than he was telling. A black cloud passed over me. For the first time I realized my brother might actually die.

"Wrap up, Feather. We need to go," Grandfather said quietly.

Mrs. Chen went to get my coat and scarf. Along with my things, she came back with a rumpled paper bag. But she gave Grandfather the bag. "Here's your order, Spotted Eagle. No charge." She gave him a very comforting, encouraging kind of smile.

"Mrs. Chen, I really must pay you for all your trouble—"

"Don't fuss. Take them," she said with a wink, "before I change my mind."

Grandfather grunted deep in his chest. "Thank you." He opened the bag. The sweet, musty odor that I smelled in the cab filled the kitchen. Then I suddenly remembered where I'd smelled it before. On Grandfather's shirts!

"May I see, Grandfather?" I asked eagerly.

"Of course, child."

I almost stuck my hand in the bag, but caught myself halfway. Grandfather nodded his approval. Instead of reaching in, however, I only peeked. The bag was full of . . . well, to be honest, it looked like a bunch of peat moss. You know, the kind you put in potted plants. I picked out a small, purplish bundle of leaves. "What's this?"

"It's sage," he answered. "Sniff."

The sage smelled good, like holiday potpourri.

"It's a sacred plant from our tribal land. It's very powerful."

I put the sage back and fished out another bundle. This one was made of braided strands of wheat-colored grass. It smelled even better than the sage, reminding me of the vanilla extract I use to make cookies. "And this one?"

"Sweetgrass. The People smudge with it. The smoke is holy. It helps purify us when we pray."

I knitted my eyebrows. "You're going to, like, smoke this?" As soon as the words were out of my mouth, I felt like an idiot.

Grandfather patiently shook his head. "No, Takoja. The People place a pinch of sweetgrass on a campfire coal. The smoke rises up to Wakan Tanka. The four-leggeds, the two-leggeds, and the winged creatures all know its fragrance. All of Mother Earth's children are thankful for sweetgrass."

"Do you, um, burn this at home sometimes? In your room?"

Grandfather grinned like he'd been caught. "Sometimes, when no one's around. Especially your practical-minded mother."

"I thought so," I winced. "I can't imagine she'd be too thrilled."

"She has plenty to learn. Just because a person doesn't believe in something doesn't mean it's not so. No matter what she thinks, the horizon of your mother's imagination is not necessarily where the sun of Truth really sets."

Across the room, Mrs. Chen chuckled.

I found one more prize in the bottom of the bag—a zip-lock freezer bag full of chopped leaves and bits of twigs. "And this?"

"Kinnikinnick."

"Pardon?"

"Red willow bark mixed with tobacco."

"For the pipe?"

"Yes, for the pipe."

I dropped the tobacco inside the paper bag and rolled the top down tight. Grandfather adjusted his hat, signaling it was time to leave. I stood up and put on my mittens.

Mrs. Chen fussed with my hat, pulling it down over my ears and tucking my scarf into my coat. "Come back and see me, Feather. And soon."

"I will. Definitely," I answered, meaning it. I stuck my hand out, but somehow a handshake didn't seem good enough to thank her for everything she'd done. I threw my arms around her.

She flashed a great big grin at me and kissed me on the cheek. "Always remember who you are, dear. Promise me you'll always remember."

"I'll remember my story, Mrs. Chen. I promise," I whispered.

Grandfather, politely acting like he wasn't listening, touched my elbow.

"Come along, Feather. It's time." He slung the pipe-case over his shoulder like a quiver of arrows.

"Goodbye, Mrs. Chen."

Mrs. Chen blew her nose in a wad of Kleenex she'd dug out of her pocket. "Goodbye, Spotted Eagle. When you have time later, let me know how Peter is doing."

Grandfather tugged the brim of his Stetson. "You know I will."

Mrs. Chen waved the handful of tissue.

Out in the store, three figures huddled by the front door. I squinted in the dark. A well-dressed Asian family stood in the flickering candlelight—a man, a woman, and a boy. They must've been waiting for us to leave. A little girl about Peter's age was collapsed in a ball in her mother's arms. Beads of sweat shone like pearls on her forehead. She shivered, and her eyes rolled back in her head. I gasped.

Grandfather stooped low, getting a good look at her. He stroked her forehead. "The person you seek is in there." He pointed at the curtain of beads. Without speaking, the family quickly disappeared through the exit.

"What do they want, Grandfather?"

"Mrs. Chen."

"But why?"

"She is one of the best herbalists around. She can do things even I don't understand."

"An h-herbalist?"

"A healer with plants. Most medicines come from plants, you know. She has the power of healing touch, too."

I remembered how warm her hands felt in the kitchen. "Could she help Peter feel better?"

"Maybe. Probably."

"Did you ask her?"

"Yes. But she says it's not that easy. She feels Peter's case is one I—or, rather, we should handle. She says it's up to us."

I chewed my lip. "Grandfather, is Peter going to be okay?"

"He is if we have anything to say about it."

There was that "we" part, again. I liked that.

CHAPTER EIGHT

Gusts of wind-driven ice smacked us in the face when Grandfather opened the door.

"Where are we going, Tunkashila?" I shouted. "To the hospital?"

"To the zoo."

I wasn't sure I'd heard him right. I couldn't have. I pushed my hat up over my ear.

"Where?"

"To the Central Park Zoo. We have an appointment with a grizzly bear."

Believe it or not, after the Mrs. Chen experience, going to the zoo to meet a bear didn't seem so unusual. I just wasn't sure what it had to do with Peter.

Grandfather looked up and down the block. For a city of millions of people, the streets were nearly empty. We were about to start walking when a solitary cab slowly rolled out of the mist. Grandfather stuck out his arm. The cab swerved to the curb.

"Wait, don't tell me," I said, "it's our friend."

The driver rolled his window down about two inches. It wasn't our friend. "Where to, Geronimo?"

Grandfather gritted his teeth. "The Central Park Zoo," he said firmly.

The driver laughed so hard he nearly swallowed the cigarette dangling from his grungy, yellow teeth. We got in the cab anyway.

The interior reeked of stale smoke. The fabric ceiling liner was shredded and the backseat was all gashed and patched with filthy duct tape. Someone had apparently tried to spit out one of the rear windows . . . and missed. "So, whadda you guys going to the zoo for in this weather? To ride the ponies?"

I rolled my eyes. Grandfather waited for the guy to quit laughing and hacking before he answered. I could tell he was getting angry. "My granddaughter and I are interested in animals."

"Yeah, ain't everybody," the cabbie snickered. Then he had another coughing attack.

Grandfather patted my hand and whispered. "Be patient, Feather. Yes, he is ignorant and impolite. But there are worse things than that. His punishment is being who he is."

The cab stopped for a red light. A grime-encrusted snowplow rumbled by. An old homeless woman dressed in a blanket and rags steered a shopping cart through the crosswalk. All of a sudden, she stopped right in front of the cab and put her hands over her eyes. I think she was trying to see who was inside.

"Move it, lady!" bellowed the cabbie. He laid on the horn.

The light changed, but the woman didn't move. She just started waving.

The driver went nuts and swiftly rolled down the window. "Beat it, you old hag, before I mash you like a bug! I mean it!"

The old woman crooked her finger at us. She apparently wanted us to get out of the cab.

"That does it!" yelled the cabbie as he started to press the accelerator.

"Stop this instant!" ordered Grandfather.

The startled driver slammed the brakes. But he was too late. His bumper hit the woman and she fell. Grandfather leapt from the car like a mountain lion. I bailed out after him.

The driver panicked. He ricocheted out of the taxi, jabbering, "It was an accident, I swear! She jumped right in front of me!"

Grandfather helped the woman to her feet, while I pushed her cart to the curb. Cars slowly pulled around the stalled taxi and started honking.

"Beat it, you rubberneckers!" yelled our driver, shaking his fist. Then, like he'd been hit by lightning, he scrambled for the cab. I guess he was making a run for it before the police arrived.

I suddenly remembered our things were still in the car. Grandfather's pipe and White Buffalo Calf Girl! My backpack and Peter's gift! "Wait!" I shouted.

The cabbie jumped in the car and started to gun the engine. I dived head first through the open backdoor, fumbling for the pipe, just as the taxi lurched forward. "Stop, you, you moron!" I screamed at the top of my lungs as the taxi skidded sideways.

The driver cursed at me and screamed: "Beat it kid! Now!"

"My pleasure," I snorted. I got out in the middle of the intersection and splashed to the curb, sinking in foot-high slush up to my ankles. At least I had our stuff.

On the corner, Grandfather waited patiently for me and extended his hand toward me. "Feather, please meet Mrs. Green."

The old woman grinned a toothless grin and stuck out her hand. She wore fingerless gloves. Her nails were so dirty you could have grown geraniums under them, and her knuckles were red and raw. The recent cold must've been murder on her.

"Sorry if I don't shake," I said. "My arms are sort of full."

She lunged and gave me a hug. A very smelly hug. I'm not sure she'd bathed since the last World Series. I didn't mind, though. It was kind of . . . I don't know . . . earthy.

"Luckily, Mrs. Green escaped serious injury," said Grandfather. He took the pipe from me.

Mrs. Green's gaze rested on my stuffed buffalo. She clicked her tongue against the roof of her mouth. "Nice, nice, n-i-c-e." Her voice was raspy as a rusty gate.

I smiled politely. When she kept staring, I got embarrassed and looked down at the pavement. She put her hands on her knees and bent down and peered up at me. Then she waved and I waved back.

Suddenly she stood up, spun around once, and started clawing at her back like she had a really bad itch. Then I saw she was untying something from around her neck. When she finally got it loose, she cupped whatever it was in both hands like you do when you catch a bug.

"Pleeese, stick out your paws, misseee," she squeaked, as she slowly opened her hands. She was holding an old quarter and a speckled pebble threaded on a piece of dirty string. "You'll need this. Wear it," she said with authority.

Afraid to argue, I bent my neck. She threw the string over my head. "Gee, thanks," I said.

"Goody, good," she said, holding up a finger and slowly twitching it under my nose. "Now everything is okay. No worries. Bye."

I had no idea what she was talking about, but before I could ask her, she waddled to her shopping cart and rummaged through its jumble of yellowed newspapers, plastic bags, and aluminum cans. I think she was taking inventory. After she was done, she rattled off down the sidewalk. When she got about thirty feet away, she stopped and turned. She cupped her hands around her mouth like a megaphone and shouted: "Say 'Hi' to my friends at the zoo."

Grandfather and I watched her until she rounded the corner. Then she was gone.

Grandfather brushed the snow off my shoulders. "I like your new necklace. It has power. It's funny, you know. The girls of the Blackfoot nation often wear stone amulets like that for luck."

I fingered my gift. A little extra luck on our journey wouldn't hurt, I thought. Peter needed it.

"Come on, we'll catch a taxi!" Grandfather called to me a few steps ahead. "We've got to hurry. We have a lot to do before dark."

Later, riding along in yet another cab, I couldn't keep my mind off Mrs. Green. "She was nice," I said out of nowhere as we bounced over a Broadway pothole.

Grandfather grunted. "That's so, Granddaughter. That's so."

"She seemed especially excited about the zoo. What did you tell her?"

"I didn't tell her about the zoo. I thought you did."

"Oh," I sighed, beginning to get used to this.

The cab bottomed out in another pothole. Just then the marquee of a passing theater burst into light. I remembered what Mrs. Chen said about everyday magic, and it made me feel happy.

CHAPTER NINE

No one was at the zoo. Not a single soul. I can't say I was surprised. The weather was miserable. In fact, the guy selling entrance tickets stared at us like we were crazy. "The Zoo's closing early today, you know. We were supposed to close an hour ago. I don't know why I haven't gotten the official word. Anyway, you better be quick."

Grandfather took the tickets. "I appreciate your concern, but we've got some important business." He tugged the brim of his hat.

I smiled. The ticket guy frowned and pulled down his window hard. Icicles drooped from the sign over the door, almost touching us, as we walked through the gates.

By the look of things, all the animals were inside their shelters. The whole place was deserted. I missed the usual chattering of monkeys and screeching of birds. Today it was completely quiet except for the soft, muffled hiss of falling snow.

Then we heard a splash. And then another! Real big splashes like when your little brother throws your sneakers in your bath just as you're about to get in. Some animals were surely around!

Grandfather lifted his chin. "Bears. Over there!"

We walked to a nearby railing and saw two polar bears wrestling in their swimming pool. What fun they were having, but then I remembered why we were here. "Are these the bears you wanted, Grandfather?"

"They are good bears, but not the ones I wanted," he answered.

"What kind are you looking for? Is something wrong with polar bears?"

He laughed. "No, there is nothing wrong with polar bears. In fact, everything is right about them. But today we are seeking someone else. We want our friend, Mato."

"Mato?"

"Mato, the grizzly bear. Mato is chief of all our four-legged relatives in regard to medicine. His strong claws are good for digging herbs. He helps us learn from Mother Earth which plants are good for fevers and which are not."

"What do we want with him?"

"I will pray for Peter. Maybe, if we are worthy, Mato will help. Maybe he will inspire a healing dream, or maybe he will help me remember a special medicine. One never knows until it happens."

I never expected Grandfather to answer that. I never expect anything Grandfather says. But I knew he was always right. I tugged his hand and looked up at him, a flake of snow hitting me in the eye. "Let's go find Mato." We started walking.

"Tunkashila?" I started to say. Somewhere in the distance a lion roared.

"Yes?"

"I've been wondering—" I searched for the right words. I couldn't find them, so I wiped my nose instead.

"What is it, Feather? Is something bothering you?"

"Not exactly. It's just that, well, is all this stuff we're doing . . . the sweetgrass, pipe, Mato . . . is it like magic?"

"That's a good question." He nodded toward the zoo's snack bar. "Come on. We'll talk about it over some hot chocolate. I want you to warm up."

I looked at my watch. Although it was only a quarter past three, it was already getting dark. From outside, the restaurant's lights glowed like candles.

Inside we took a seat at a small, round table. The lady behind the register had her eyes glued to us like we were about to swipe the napkin dispenser or something. Maybe she was just lonely for some company. We were the only two customers. While Grandfather got the hot chocolate, I called Emily. I pulled my mittens off with my teeth, turned on my cell and punched buttons. The phone rang three times, four times . . . more. "Come on, be there," I muttered.

Finally, Emily answered. "Hello?"

"Guess where I am."

"At home?"

"Not even close. Guess again."

"The hospital, visiting Peter?"

"Not even warm."

"Who am I, Feather, Madame Zelda the mind reader?"

"Come on, be a sport, Em. Guess!"

"You're at the track."

"Very funny, Emily. Really! Guess! You'll never believe it. Not in a million years."

Now Emily has a very active imagination … and that's putting it mildly. I think her parents had her tested by a psychologist one time or something. She reacted true to form.

"Omigod! You're being held hostage! The kidnappers made up that Peter was sick to lure you from school! I bet you're trying to tell me where you are! Okay, okay, be calm. Give me a hint. How many syllables?"

"Emily! Chill! Everything's okay. We're at the zoo."

"Yeah, right, the zoo. I get it. Sure." Then she whispered, "So the first word starts with 'z' right? Let's see—"

"Please, Em. I'm serious."

She was disappointed. "Oh. You are serious. What are you doing there?"

"I can't explain right now. But I think we're going to the hospital next. Peter isn't doing too well."

"I'm sorry," Emily said. I knew she meant it. "Wait, who's 'we'?"

"Grandfather came to the school office and got me. Don't ask. What's going on? How was school?"

"Great! They let us out early because of the weather. For your information, Billy Braslau asked where you were—wait, why is the zoo still open?"

I ignored her last question and thought of Billy Braslau. He's exceptionally cute. Nice curly, brown hair, big smile, great eyes, and dimples. This was an interesting development, but I didn't have time to deal with it. "Look, I gotta go. Camp out by the phone. I'll call you when I get to the hospital."

"Uh, Feather?"

I didn't like the sound of that. "Yes?"

"I almost forgot. One more thing. Your mother called a minute ago. She's looking for you."

This was not good news. I looked down at my phone. She was right. I had a message. Apparently, Mom had called when my phone was turned off. "What did you tell her?"

"What could I do? I said I didn't know where you were."

"Great! Couldn't you lie for once! She probably thinks I'm dead or something!"

Emily coughed. "Gee, Feather. I'm sorry."

"No, really, I'm the one that should be sorry," I replied. "I shouldn't snap at you. Just hang on to your phone. Don't lose it like you usually do. I'll call as soon as I can."

"Affirmative! I'll sit on my phone like an ostrich hatching an egg!"

"That sounds painful, Emily. Goodbye."

"Bye. Feather?"

"Yes?"

"Take care of yourself. Seriously."

"I will. Seriously. And, hey, Em—"

"What?"

"You're the best friend a girl could have. Seriously."

She laughed. "I know. Bye."

I returned to the table just as Grandfather came back with two large cocoas. Steam boiled out when he removed the plastic lids. He took a sip and grimaced like he had a toothache. "Ah, just right."

He took another sip. I didn't dare touch mine yet. Nothing's worse than scalded tongue. He rubbed his hands together. "Feels nice to be indoors, doesn't it?"

"It sure does," I said, feeling the warmth of the place envelop me. I took off my coat.

Grandfather noisily swallowed more cocoa. "Ahh, that's good. Almost as good as my coffee." He looked at some posters on a nearby wall featuring the usual suspects: a koala, a lioness, a baby gorilla, a zebra, and, of course, a panda. Adults always think kids are nuts over pandas.

Then Grandfather pulled out a red bandanna and blew his nose. As he stuffed the cloth back in his pocket, he said, "A minute ago you were asking me if what we are doing is magic."

"Is it? Because, you know, quite frankly, I wondered. You know how Mom is. She'll make fun of us. Not that I care, really." I took a sip of hot chocolate and shifted in my seat.

"What do you think, Feather? Do you think it's magic?"

I didn't answer.

He pointed to the posters. "Are they magic?"

I took another sip of cocoa and sniffed. "The animals? No, they're real."

Grandfather chuckled. "Well, let me rephrase the matter, Feather. What we're doing is not magic. It's not cheap card tricks or spooky Halloween business. Think about it this way. How does a caterpillar change into a butterfly?"

I shrugged my shoulders. "Heck, I don't know."

"You're not alone. No one knows for sure. You see, Takoja, the things we're doing are things the People learned from Mother Earth thousands of years ago. They are natural, and, just like butterflies, they are mysterious and must be respected. But, no, they are not magic. Satisfied?"

"Yeah," I said. "I am."

Grandfather chewed his thumbnail. "Oh, by the way, how was Emily?"

"Fine—hey! How did you know I called her?"

"Lucky guess," he answered. He drank more cocoa and wiped his mouth on the back of his hand. When he saw I noticed, he smiled. "I know, I know. I should use a napkin."

I took a sip and wiped my mouth on the back of my hand just like he did. "Wait, no way. How could you possibly know I called Emily?"

Grandfather just laughed again. "Finish your cocoa. We have an appointment with a grizzly bear."

When we got there, every last one of the bear habitats was empty. Well, except for the polar bears. They were thrilled by the awful weather. The other bears were all inside.

We read the sign in front of the grizzly showcase. A map showed where grizzlies used to live in the wild and where they live now. Not many places today. I could tell Grandfather was disappointed our particular bear was missing. Peter needed help. Grandfather bowed his head and whispered in Lakota.

"What are you saying, Grandfather?"

"The words to a bear song I learned when I was a little boy. It goes 'My paw is sacred. All things are sacred.'" He sighed. "People can learn a lot from bears."

As a final offering, he grabbed a pinch of pipe tobacco and threw it in the bear pen. "We cannot see you, Mato, but we know you are here. Thank you."

I snapped my fingers. "Wait a minute, Tunkashila! I have an idea!"

I told him about a film Emily and I saw at school called *After Hours at the Zoo*. I remembered a scene showing some secret tunnels behind the open-air displays that allowed the zookeepers to shovel food to the animals without being seen by the public. All we had to do was find one of these tunnels and our problem was solved. Instant bear!

Grandfather thought a minute. He rubbed his chin. "Well, I would like to see a bear."

"Follow me!" I exclaimed, sure that I would find a way.

It didn't take long. Behind the panda exhibit, we found a gray steel door with the words "ZOO PERSONNEL ONLY" neatly stenciled on it in white paint.

"This must be the place," I whispered. I looked around to make sure the coast was clear. The only other people I saw were halfway across the zoo, trudging through the snow toward the exit. I tried the door. We were in luck. It was unlocked! I held my breath and eased it open.

Just then an angry voice shouted just as we were heading inside. "Hey, you two! Where do you think you're going?" We were busted.

CHAPTER TEN

"Not so fast!" ordered a hatchet-faced security guard. "Can't you two Einsteins read?" He jabbed a gloved thumb at the door, slid back the hood of his parka and smirked at me. "Cat got your tongue?" He noticed White Buffalo Calf Girl. "Nice dolly," he said with sarcasm. Then he glared at Grandfather. "Okay, Chief, what gives?"

Grandfather slowly raised his right hand. "How." I tried not to laugh.

The guard's jaw fell open. After he recovered, he blared, "Who the heck are you supposed to be, Chief? Sitting Bull?"

Grandfather didn't utter a peep.

Realizing he was getting nowhere, the guard turned his attention to me. He bent down, and I knew he definitely had garlic for lunch. "Okay, kiddo, what gives? Come on, let's have it." He certainly seemed convinced I'd tell him what he wanted to hear.

I had an idea. I held my hands limply over my head, stuck out my lower lip, and went "Oooh, Oooh, Oooh." Then I scratched under my arms. Luckily, the guard got it. I mean, how hard was it?

"You wanna see the monkeys, kid? For Pete's sake, why didn't you say so!" He pointed. "Look it, you go that way. Turn the corner by the giraffes and go straight. Only an idiot could miss them. The smell alone will knock you down. But be quick because we're closing soon!"

I pumped the guard's hand up and down like I was jacking up a car to fix a flat tire and then led Grandfather away.

"Foreigners! Go figure," the guard muttered, shaking his head.

As we turned the corner by the giraffe area, I looked back to check on the guard who was still standing there. I waved. He didn't. In a minute, after we caught our breath, I stuck my head back around the corner. The guard was gone.

I grabbed Grandfather's hand. "Let's go find us a bear, Tunkashila!" We made a beeline for the door. When we got there, I took a deep breath and swung it open. We stepped into a brightly lit hallway. Its tile wall and floor were scrubbed sparkling and smelled of Pine-Sol. Steel doors lined the hall. Each door had a small window. I looked in the first one.

"What do you see?" asked Grandfather.

I stood on my tiptoes. "Nothing but an empty cage."

He peered in the window across the hall.

"Whatcha got?" I asked, knowing he found something.

"Bears," he replied with relief. "Come see."

He gave me a boost. Two baby black bears huddled next to their sleeping mother. One of the babies saw me. She lifted her head and yawned. Her tiny tongue was pinker than Barbie's Dream House. I waved at her. She yawned again and flopped on her back.

"Cute, but not who we want," I said. "Let's try another one."

Grandfather used his hands to make a stirrup for me to stand in. There was nothing through the first window and nothing through the one across the hall, either. Nothing but fluorescent lights, an empty cage, and a blue plastic bucket. A mop stood in the corner.

There were four windows left. Two on each side of the hall. Three times Grandfather boosted me and three times I had to say, "Nothing."

"Are you sure? Check all the corners," he suggested after the third try. He wanted that bear to be there more than anything. So did I.

I smashed my nose against the cold glass. Maybe she was there. Maybe I hadn't tried hard enough. "More of the same. Empty," I finally sighed, sliding to the floor through Grandfather's hands. I could feel his arms trembling as he set me down. He was real tired now.

One chance remained, and so he started to give me another boost up.

"You've done enough," I stopped him. "I'll do it myself."

This time, something was different from the start. The window was smudged. Somebody else's nose other than mine had pressed against it. I felt funny. A bear was in there. I don't know how I knew, but I knew. I stretched on my tiptoes.

Darkness loomed on the other side of the pane. I cupped my hands to the side of my face. Pitch black faded into shades of gray. Shapes appeared. I saw a big aluminum bowl on the floor and a fat tractor tire hanging by a rope from the ceiling. Almost out of my sight, far to the left, was a wall of black. I wondered if something was there. I stared hard.

The blackness moved. Maybe I was seeing things. I rubbed a fist in my eye.

There it was again. Movement. Barely up and down. Up and down like the ocean—or someone breathing. I pounded on the glass.

Grandfather grabbed my wrist. "Takoja, what are you doing?"

"Look, Grandfather! Look! See for yourself!" I exclaimed louder than I should have, considering we were trespassing.

Grandfather took off his cowboy hat and mashed his face against the glass. He kept it there a long time. Finally, he shook his head. "I'm afraid I can't see anything, Takoja. My eyes are old. Yours are young. You have to see for me."

I took another look. Nearly everything was dark. But one spot was darker, and it moved. It was alive. "There's a bear in there, all right," I said with excitement. I twisted the doorknob, but it didn't budge.

"Try this," said Grandfather, giving me his bone-handled pocketknife.

I jiggled the blade in the lock. That didn't work. I shoved it deeper.

"Don't force it," said Grandfather. "Let the knife find its way."

Suddenly the outside door flew open, ushering in a blast of cold air. Grandfather and I went still. A zookeeper stood in the doorway.

Despite being camouflaged by a bulky parka, green coveralls and black rubber boots, she appeared to be young, probably fresh out of college. Her cheeks were cherry red from the cold. Before she could spot us, she propped the door open with a boot and shouted back over her shoulder at someone outside. She was pushing a surprisingly large wheelbarrow.

Red meat chunks, marbled thick with greasy, white fat and heaps of wilted lettuce filled the wheelbarrow. It was feeding time.

Luckily, she kept arguing with whoever was outside. I hoped it wasn't our friend the security guard. But that didn't matter. The main thing was that she still hadn't seen us. Yet.

Like startled deer caught in the headlights of an onrushing eighteen-wheeler, Grandfather and I stood paralyzed. I wondered if Mom would bail us out at the police station, which was where we were undoubtedly headed.

Meanwhile, the young zookeeper kept arguing with the person outside. "Oh, all right. Don't be such a baby. I'll give you a hand," she finally surrendered in exasperation to her co-worker waiting outside. She didn't seem too pleased. She flicked her long, blonde ponytail and disdainfully muttered, "I've never heard of anyone who was scared of a llama!"

I slowly exhaled. We were safe. But for how long? I wiggled the knife in the lock like my life depended on it. With a *snick*, the knob turned. Packages and all,

Grandfather and I squeezed through the door. We weren't alone. Lost in the darkness, somebody was snoring.

"Mato," whispered Grandfather.

"What do we do now?" I whispered back.

"I need to pray a little. Then Mato will help me think about how to help Peter. That's about it. Then we can go."

"I'll be the lookout," I offered in a loud whisper.

Grandfather patted my shoulder. "Smell him?"

I sniffed. A flat, musty smell tickled my nose. It smelled like a garden, earthy and kind of stinky. It smelled like a bear.

The snoring mound moved up and down with every breath. Mato was only three feet away, and she was enormous! I could've touched her . . . if I wanted to.

I blended into the shadows by the door and peeped out the window. The hall was empty. I pressed my ear against the cool glass. I couldn't hear anything.

Grandfather raised his arms and prayed aloud in Lakota. Then he bent down on one knee and opened the paper sack. The bear snuffled and licked her lips. When her snoring resumed, he took out the tobacco pouch and poured some flakes in his palm. He prayed some more and threw pinches of tobacco to the four directions, thanking Mato the bear for her help. Then Grandfather rose to his feet with finality. We were done.

All of a sudden, the room exploded with light. Grandfather hunched his shoulders like a boxer taking a punch. Spots swam before my eyes like fat albino guppies. Down the hall, a door slammed. The zookeeper was back. She'd obviously turned on the overhead lights in the cages. She was the least of my worries right now, however. The bear was awake.

Golden brown fur, the color of honey, pressed against the bars. I heard a tremendous yawn and then the brown fur jerkily squashed back and forth against the bars. She was scratching her back!

Grandfather held up his hand, cautioning me not to move.

Her back to the cage bars, the bear sat up on her bottom with her feet splayed out in front of her. She yawned again. I caught a glimpse of purple gums and white teeth. That's when I noticed her claws. Sharp, ivory-colored claws shaped like crescent moons. She sniffed the air, sucking it in like she was tasting it. She went completely still when she realized she wasn't alone.

Quicker than a cat can lick its paw, the bear wheeled and stood on her hind legs. It seemed she'd never stop rising, taller and taller. I thought she was going to go through the ceiling. She was beautiful. Like a mountain is beautiful. And awesome. I was riveted to the floor.

She blinked at us like she couldn't quite believe we were there. She shook her head.

"Kodiak," Grandfather whispered.

"Kodak?" I asked out of the side of my mouth, not taking my eyes off her. "Like the camera?" My voice sounded a little shaky. It was amazing I could speak at all.

"Kodiak Island, Alaska," Grandfather was saying. "The brown bears from there are related to grizzlies, only they're bigger. She's a prime Kodiak." He sighed in awe, softly whistling between his teeth.

The bear wasn't sure what to do about us. A grumbling sound like a passing freight train filled the room. I hoped she was saying "Hello."

Grandfather chanted in Lakota. The bear cocked her head and stared at him like she was working hard to translate whatever he was saying into bear talk. Then she plopped right down on her wide bottom.

"I thanked her for her hospitality," whispered Grandfather. "I think she'd like us to stay, but I told her we had to get going—"

Down the hall, a door slammed.

"—and soon," he added.

"Is she going to help us with Peter?"

"She already has," Grandfather said quietly, "although I wish I had some of that." He pointed to the cage bars.

"What?"

"Fur."

"Where? Besides all over her, I mean."

"There, on the bars. She shed some during her backrub."

I squinted. "Oh, what do you want it for?"

He adjusted his Stetson. "Keep some for my medicine bag. Take a little Mato medicine with me. It might help Peter. Who knows, it might help all of us."

"Are you going to take some? Do you think she'll let you go near her?"

"I don't think it's wise to get too close. She's a nursing mother with cubs."

This was news. I hadn't seen the babies. Sure enough, there they were, the color of gold, curled around one another, nearly hidden in a pile of wheat-colored straw.

What I did next was really stupid. But it's not like I thought about it. I just did it. In two steps, I was at the bars. The bear lumbered to her feet, watching me closely. Her amber eyes looked straight into mine. She snuffled at me and licked her lips.

Grandfather didn't make a sound. I imagine he thought I was going to be eaten alive.

"Please, may I?" I asked her. The bear sniffed some more. Slowly, and very, very carefully, I collected a handful of soft fur. Quicker than I could see, she leaned down...and licked my hand. Her tongue felt like a warm washcloth. When she was done, I walked backwards to Grandfather and gave him the fur.

His face was shining. "Hoka Hey!" he exclaimed with enthusiasm, giving the old Lakota war cry. "You're a brave one, Takoja!" He wrapped the fur in his bandanna.

I waved to the bear. "Bye. Take care of the kids . . . and thanks!"

The bear sat down, shook her massive head, and lazily scratched her ribs like a toddler just up from her nap.

At that moment the door right across the hall slammed.

"We better get going," whispered Grandfather. He collected our belongings while I picked up White Buffalo Calf Girl.

"How are we going to do this without getting caught?" I asked.

"We'll walk out of here like we own the place. Courage is better than cowardice," he explained. "Always." Then he opened the door for me. "After you," he said graciously.

I stepped into the hall. Not three feet away the pretty zookeeper was bent over her wheelbarrow, balancing a pitchfork loaded with cabbages. She gaped at us like we were Martians.

Grandfather tipped his hat. "Good afternoon."

As I passed I smiled at her and waved. "Bye! We adored the tour!"

Her mouth fell open as she stood there gaping at us. She was too shocked to say anything. And I think she'd already had a pretty long day by the look of things.

Grandfather and I made a beeline for the gate.

CHAPTER ELEVEN

W e stopped to catch our breath under General Sherman's gleaming gold-leaf statue at the edge of Central Park. It had stopped snowing while we were in the zoo and the sky was clearing now. A thin band of baby blue showed along the horizon and the buildings lining the park's east side glowed orange and purple in the sunset like desert cliffs. Behind us the park was quiet, insulated by the icy pelt that smoothed its surface into a frozen white sea. Rush hour was going on full-blast. A honking river of cars, buses, taxis, and trucks clotted the streets and people poured from the surrounding offices like spilling birdseed.

Grandfather calmly walked over to the Fifth Avenue curb and stuck out his arm. Although the chances of getting a cab looked awfully slim, one immediately responded. I shook my head, wondering how he did it.

Before the taxi's wheels stopped rolling, its back door burst open and identical twin girls wearing plaid school uniforms and red berets emerged with a whoop. Their flustered mother threw some loose change at the driver and set off in pursuit.

We watched them melt into the crowd. Grandfather smiled. "Good omen. Happy kids are always a good sign."

When we got in the taxi, Grandfather tapped the driver on the shoulder. "Fifth Avenue and Thirty-Fourth Street, please."

"We're going to the hospital, finally?" I knew that my friend Emily would never be as patient as I, but then she didn't know Grandfather like I did. I had complete faith in him.

Grandfather shook his head. "No. Not yet. We're heading to the high country." He nodded toward the glass canyons of midtown Manhattan where the tightly-packed skyscrapers glowed like fireflies.

"The high country? You've lost me again, Tunkashila."

"You'll see, don't worry. Simply be open to what is about to happen."

I wasn't sure what to make of that last part, but at least it sounded interesting.

After the driver wrote down the destination that Grandfather gave her, she smacked a big wad of gum and said, "You got it, handsome. The high country." Her bright red fingernails clicked on the steering wheel when she pulled into traffic. She caught me watching her in the rearview mirror. She hitched up the shoulders of her leather bomber jacket.

"Hiya, kid."

I smiled and looked away. The driver turned on the radio and started singing along to a country and western song. I liked her.

When we bounced over an enormous moon crater of a pothole at the intersection of Fifth and Fifty-Sixth Street, Grandfather patted my knee. "So, what do you think so far?"

"I'm having a great time!" I exclaimed. Then I remembered Peter. Every once in awhile I'd remember Peter, usually at moments when I was most excited. Again I felt bad, but then I thought of Grandfather and my complete faith in him. He knew what he was doing, even if I didn't. And we were on a mission precisely for Peter.

"This reminds me of why I came to New York," Grandfather said thoughtfully.

"Why, Tunka?"

He gestured toward the window. "Look there."

I looked where he pointed. The sidewalks were swollen with people. All kinds of people from every corner of the globe. Wrapped up against the freezing cold, walking with their heads down, lost in their own private worlds. On and on they went. Hundreds of them.

"The people are why I came to New York. All the two-leggeds. May Creator and Mother Earth bless them. I brought your mother to the city when she was a teenager, not much older than you are now."

This was one story I hadn't heard before. My ears perked up. "Why, Grandfather?"

"Because she was so smart and eager to learn. I thought she could find something here she couldn't find on the reservation."

He winced, as if the memory hurt. "Your grandmother had just died. Your mother and I were alone in the world, and just as she was ready to start high school. Before, she was bright and ready for anything, like a young otter pup. The loss of her mother crushed her. She became bitter and angry. She even ran away from home once. She stayed with a friend in Bismarck, North Dakota, for three days before I found her."

I'd never heard anything about that running away part. I couldn't imagine old Mom the control freak doing anything so wild and unpredictable. I listened for more details.

"I was worried. And scared. I didn't know what to do for her. After all she was my baby, my pride and joy, born when I was forty years old." He stroked his chin and stared out the window. "At the time the reservation was in a bad way. The outside world had forgotten about us. I think maybe they just wanted the Indians to go away."

He smacked a fist into his palm. I flinched. The driver stopped singing and turned the radio down low. I could tell she was eavesdropping.

"The proud Lakota people, the people who once lived in their painted lodges on the prairie as free children of Mother Earth, had come to live in tar paper shacks and tumble-down log cabins. Some even slept in rusted-out abandoned automobiles. You can't imagine it. Many were sick, hungry, and dying of drink." Grandfather paused.

I held my breath.

"I knew your mother needed help. I'd been in New York many times when I was a sailor. I knew it was a good place. It had art museums, and libraries, and music, any kind of music. And it was far from the reservation. So I moved her here."

For a couple of blocks, he was silent. Then he picked up where he left off.

"In the city your mother came back to life. She loved high school, and the proudest day of my life was when she was accepted at Columbia. She's made a heck of a good lawyer, too. But deep inside I think she still hurts badly. I pray for her every day." He turned his face to the window.

I touched his hand. "You did the right thing, Grandfather. She knows you love her."

He gave a little laugh. "I've tried."

The traffic crept along like a half-hearted caterpillar. Stop. Start. Stop. Start. It was almost dark. When the taxi moved shadows rolled across Grandfather's face in waves.

"There is one thing I regret," he added. "And I've never told anyone. I regret . . . I regret that somewhere along the way your mother stopped being an Indian. Not because she wanted to, but because she felt she had to. The life she left behind was one of utter despair. She shed herself of it completely, like a traveler shakes dust from her feet."

I could feel how hard it was for him to reveal this, and I hurt for him.

"After law school she cast aside the traditional beliefs of her ancestors. I suppose they reminded her too much of the past. She remembers only the material poverty of her childhood, not the spiritual riches that have enabled our people to survive." He waved his hand before his eyes like he was brushing away cobwebs. "The horror of it, Feather, the absolute horror of it, is that I feel I'm responsible. I wasn't a good enough example. I didn't live out the old ways in a manner which would show her how important they are to—"

"Oh, Grandfather, don't say that, please," I protested. "You know that's not true."

"But don't you see, Takoja. There is a wound in her heart I can't heal. Me, a medicine man, and I can't even help my own daughter. Worst of all, she knows it. She thinks I'm only a superstitious old fool. That's why she won't let me help Peter. Sometimes I'm afraid she may be right."

"That's not true at all!" I exclaimed.

He turned away, but I grabbed his arm. "Look at me!"

Grandfather stared at me in surprise. So did the cabbie, who suddenly twisted around like a pretzel. The cab swerved toward the oncoming stream of headlights.

"Not you!" I shouted. I took a big breath and tried to calm down. "Tunkashila, please," I pleaded. "Mom just doesn't understand. Maybe someday she will. Maybe someday she'll get her story back. Like you did. But she has to do it on her own. Don't give up on her."

He was listening. I kept going. "I understand you. And I believe in you. I know you can help Peter."

His eyes filled with light.

"And you know what else?"

"What, Takoja?"

"I love you." I threw my arms around his neck.

The cab braked and lurched to the curb. The driver blew her nose into a Kleenex. "You guys choke me up," she spluttered. She daubed under her eyes, tie-dyeing the tissue black with mascara. "I'm a sucker for a sob story." She blew her nose again, honking like a foghorn. "Here you are—Fifth and Thirty-Fourth. And I ain't chargin' you guys nuthin'. I ain't had a good cry like this in ages."

Grandfather and I both thanked the cabbie. I even leaned over the front seat and gave her a hug. Then I wiped the condensation off the window with my elbow and peered out. We were parked right in front of the Empire State Building.

CHAPTER TWELVE

*T*he Empire State Building. So that's what Grandfather meant when he said we were going to the "high country." As I got out of the cab, I craned my neck to look up. I remembered what Grandfather said about seeking visions on the mountaintop. All of a sudden I had a funny feeling in the pit of my stomach.

Before we went indoors, we stood beneath the entrance awning and watched a flood of briefcase-toting adults flee the building. While we waited for the professional tide to go down, Grandfather tried to prepare me for what was coming next.

"Feather, everything we've done today has been in preparation for this moment. You may not understand everything we do, but don't be afraid. Understanding has its place, but some things are beyond mere understanding. They're greater than that. They can only be felt in the heart."

He took the pipecase off his shoulder. "For hundreds of years, whenever they were happy and whenever they were in need, our Lakota people prayed with their sacred pipes. Today, Feather, for the first time, you will follow in the footsteps of your ancestors." Then he craned his neck back and looked up at the top of the Empire State Building. "On this lonely mountaintop, they, and all they stood for, will live in you."

Driven by a whistling north wind, the awning snapped and popped. Grandfather held the pipe aloft and its feathers rustled and then expanded in front of my eyes like a Japanese paper fan. His voice soared like a hawk above the deep rush-hour rumble. "Every day we draw breath we should walk in joy, with our feet on Mother Earth and our hearts reaching toward the stars. We should greet the four-legged and the winged peoples as our sisters and brothers. We should care for the forests and the rivers as we care for members of our own family. When we live this way, my granddaughter, the Creator is happy, and the earth, the sky, and all living beings are one, and the great hoop of life is complete."

He lowered the pipe and held it in front of me like an offering. "Given to us by White Buffalo Calf Girl on that wonderful day so long ago, the sacred pipe is our guide on this holy path. When we respect it and use it wisely, it brings harmony, hope, and healing. And so we must use my own medicine pipe today to help Peter, if we can." He paused. "Does this make sense to you?"

I nodded. "Yes, Grandfather, it makes sense to me, more than anything."

Love and pride creased his face. "I thought it would. Come on, it's time to begin."

Entering the lobby we dodged some people headed out of the building, and then made our way over to the elevator banks. While waiting for one of the elevators to open, Grandfather reached in his coat pocket and took out a little porcelain jar. To me, it looked like lip gloss. When the elevator arrived, we got on alone.

As soon as the doors shut, Grandfather unscrewed the lid on the little jar and stuck two fingertips into the thick cream inside. Checking his reflection in the polished elevator doors, he spread the white goo from ear to ear across the bridge of his nose. It definitely wasn't lip gloss—it was face paint! He screwed the lid back on the jar and wiped his hands on his bandanna. He winked at me. "Now I really look like an Indian."

I gave him a "thumbs up" and punched the elevator button. Soon Fifth Avenue was a thousand feet below us. As we were lifted upward, I felt my stomach drop to the floor. Finally we arrived at the top floor. Straight ahead on the far wall, a sign read "WELCOME TO THE OBSERVATORY. OPEN DAILY 9:30 A.M. TO MIDNIGHT. $3.50 FOR ADULTS, $1.75 CHILDREN UNDER TWELVE." The hallway was empty, which wasn't too surprising, considering the weather. We went to the window where we had to pay.

The ticket lady didn't look up. She held a tattered copy of *Cosmopolitan* in front of her like she was studying for a really hard test. Her name tag read "Yvonne." A boom box played easy listening music in the background. We waited politely. Yvonne didn't notice us. Grandfather coughed. Yvonne looked up and saw Grandfather's painted face and screamed.

Before Grandfather could reassure her, Yvonne jackknifed in her swivel chair and sprinted for the back of the office. She was going so fast that she broke a heel off her pumps as she cornered the last desk between her and the door.

Grandfather shook his head.

Pretty soon a bald-headed guy peeked around the same door. Like a moonrise, out came his head, smooth and creamy like an egg. Then came his eyebrows, bushy and black. Then came his eyes, beady and brown. He saw Grandfather. Up went his eyebrows. Back went his head. We heard a lot of whispering.

The whispering stopped, and the owner of the bald head appeared. He looked a little rattled. His name tag read "Larry."

"May I h-help you?" he asked nervously.

"Yes, sir," Grandfather replied, "my granddaughter and I would like to go out and enjoy the view."

Larry inspected us. "How old is she?" he asked.

"Almost twelve," I answered.

Larry looked at me and then, really quickly, right back at Grandfather like he was afraid to take his eyes off him. "Eleven," said Larry. "So that's one adult and one child. Five twenty-five, please."

Grandfather pushed the money over the counter. Larry stared at it like it was radioactive. "Right," he said. Then he stuffed it in the cash register without looking down.

Grandfather thanked him and turned to leave.

"Wait a minute, s-sir. You gotta check all those p-packages," Larry said, trying his best to sound tough. To be honest, he was having a hard time. His voice kept cracking.

Grandfather looked him in the eye. "These are valuable personal belongings. Family heirlooms, you might say. I appreciate your concern, though. I know you're only doing your job."

Larry swallowed so hard his Adam's apple bounced. "Well, okay, but you two better not try any funny business or I'll have to call security."

Grandfather put Peter's present on the counter and swung the pipecase off his shoulder. Larry ducked under the counter and shrieked, "Don't shoot! I'm a family man!"

"Please, friend, I meant no harm," Grandfather said reassuringly, leaning over the counter. "Please come out. I only wanted to show you what we're carrying."

Larry stood up, quivering like a Chihuahua on a latte binge.

"Don't be scared. See?" said Grandfather as he opened the paper bag.

Larry licked his lips and peeked in the sack like he expected to see an iguana or something. But he grinned with relief when he saw what it really contained. "Groceries, huh?"

"In a manner of speaking," replied Grandfather. He shook the present. "And a fire engine for my grandson."

Larry inspected the wrapper. "FAO Schwarz. My kids love that place."

"How many children do you have, if I may ask?"

"Three. All girls. All brilliant," Larry whistled, shaking his head. He took out his billfold and showed Grandfather a picture. "This one plays varsity basketball." He tapped the photo proudly.

"They're handsome," said Grandfather. He took out the pipe. Larry's eyes bulged.

"Wow!" he gulped. "May I touch it?"

Grandfather held the pipe in both hands. Larry ran his pinkie down the stem.

"I've never seen one of these before. I mean, you know, not in real life. It's awesome."

"Thank you, Larry. If you don't mind, my grand-daughter and I will go outside now," said Grandfather, as he slipped the pipe back into its case.

Larry saluted. "Great! Enjoy yourselves," he beamed. He was a new man.

"That sure was nice," I told Grandfather on our way outside. "But you know, I'm kind of surprised you let him touch the pipe. I mean—it's so special and all."

Grandfather rubbed the top of my head. "Usually, I wouldn't, Takoja. The pipe is not for those whose eyes can't see and whose hearts can't feel."

"But then, well, why Larry?"

"Granddaughter, the path of the heart is the best. It's also the hardest. Many people choose the easy paths of power, pride, or intolerance. When I heard the love in Larry's voice when he mentioned his children, I knew he walked the right path. He was worthy."

"What about Yvonne? Is she a good person, too?"

"One of the best, I bet." He pushed his cowboy hat down over his eyes. "Now let's go pray for Peter in the old way."

I opened the outside door and peered to the right and the left. No one was around. Grandfather and I had the entire observatory to ourselves. We walked to the railing, scrunching ice under our feet. A cold wind rushed up the side of the building and lashed our hair in our faces. Below us lay all New York, powdered white with snow. Square in the middle of the city, Central Park sat like a frosted cupcake. The lights of the Bronx and Queens blinked in the distance.

I took a deep breath. Nestled somewhere among the forest of concrete and steel at my feet was the hospital where Peter was fighting for his life. I hoped whatever Grandfather had in mind would help. Most of all, I prayed it wasn't too late.

Grandfather and I took in the view. It sure seemed like you could see forever. In the twilight, skyscrapers sparkled all around us like fallen stars. Above the wrinkled New Jersey cliffs across the Hudson, a red sun sagged like a tired party guest. We were all by ourselves. Only a couple that looked like college kids with long scarves and knit hats were around, and they seemed to be leaving at that moment.

After a minute Grandfather cleared his throat. "Before we start, Feather, I want you to shut your eyes and look with your heart. I want you to see what this land was like many years ago."

Listening to him, I closed my eyes.

"Instead of apartment blocks full of frightened strangers, imagine tipi circles full of strong and happy families. Feel yourself surrounded by rustling cotton-wood trees, not office towers. Instead of automobiles picture mountain lions roaming free."

I crunched my eyes tighter, concentrating on the picture Grandfather painted.

"Above your head don't envision jets groaning towards La Guardia Airport, but soaring red-tailed hawks. See clear, trout-filled streams crossing the land, not ribbons of asphalt. Instead of wailing sirens the cries of eagles fill your ears. And the scent of an alpine meadow, not bus exhaust, tickles your nose. This land was once such sacred ground."

He put his lips almost to my ear. "My granddaughter, believe that you are not atop this pile of bricks, but on a lonely mountaintop. Believe that you are an Indian girl begging for a vision to heal her people."

I kept my eyes tightly shut. "I'm trying hard, Grandfather."

"Don't try, Feather. Simply open your heart and it will come to you."

I quit trying and let my mind go blank. Gradually the cold and the noise of the city faded away. Suddenly like a camera focusing, there I was standing on a mountaintop, gazing out over the prairie with my hair flowing freely, not trapped under an itchy wool hat. Instead of my jacket, scarf, and boots, I wore a soft buckskin dress and fur-lined moccasins. Below me, a chestnut sea of buffalo thundered over the rolling plains and an eagle circled overhead. I felt wonderful and I felt free. I was where I belonged.

"I'm there, Grandfather!" I cried. As soon as the words were out of my mouth, the image popped like a soap bubble. I stomped my foot. "Lost it!"

"No, Feather, you didn't lose it. It's yours forever. For that's the world your ancestors lived in. They loved the earth. She was their mother and they were her children. And it was good."

He put his hand on my shoulder. "Now open your eyes."

I blinked. The brutal wind whipping around the ledge made my eyes water.

"What do you see?"

"The city. Buildings, lots of lights, bridges, cars."

"What do you hear?"

I listened. "Taxis honking, sirens, a car alarm."

"There's a difference, then, between your inner and outer visions?"

"A big difference."

"How does that make you feel?"

"Sort of sad, I guess."

Grandfather turned away from me and looked out over the city.

I started to really feel the cold now. The temperature was dropping faster than the sun.

Grandfather sighed. "You're not alone. I think a lot of people are sad these days. But let me ask you. Why do you feel sad?"

"Well, I don't know," I answered, thinking about it a moment. "I guess, because that beautiful place—the place where I was—is only make-believe. It's not real. It's only a dream."

"If that was a dream, then this must be a nightmare." He motioned over the city. "Look around, and what do you see? Everywhere around us are drugs, guns, disease, war, and racism. Children being hurt and families torn apart. People without food, people without homes, people without useful work, without even a clean cup of water for their little ones."

He shook his head sadly.

"Everyday you see the skies above and the seas below being poisoned. You see the earth, our mother, being smothered in concrete and our four-legged brothers and sisters being chased and destroyed. Yet they are conscious beings that feel pain and fear just like we do. And do you know why this is so?"

"No, Tunkashila."

"Because the old ways are forgotten. The sacred Circle of Life is broken. People are lost. They're like sleepwalkers who can't remember the way home."

"Where is home, Grandfather?"

"It's where you just were, Feather. Home is that mountaintop in your heart where you are known and loved and accepted. Home is where you are a child of Wakan Tanka and Mother Earth, and a sister to all living beings. That is your true home and the most real place of all."

The wind howled like a living thing. I pulled my hat low over my ears and started to shiver. "Would you like to go back to that mountaintop, Feather? Would you like to go there and say a prayer for Peter with me in the old Lakota way?"

"Yes, Tunkashila, more than anything." I forgot about the cold at that moment. And I even stopped shivering.

"Good, my granddaughter. And one more thing. Will you promise me something?"

"Yes, Tunka. You know I'll do anything for you."

"Will you always remember what I've taught you, so that after I am gone you can lead your people and show the lost ones the way home?"

"Lost ones? Like Mom?"

"Yes, Feather, her and anyone else who needs help. As a medicine woman, all the people of the world shall be your family."

"A medicine woman?"

"It's your destiny. A dream told me it was time for you to know. That is what our adventures today have been about, too. We're not only trying to save Peter, we're also bringing a new healer into the world. You."

I gasped and looked up at him. A tear ran down his cheek.

"Will you lead your people, my granddaughter? Will you show them the way home?"

I felt like I could fly. "I promise, Grandfather!"

Right there atop of the Empire State Building, I kissed my grandfather on the cheek and told him I loved him. And all around the wind howled wildly, as if the mighty white wolf herself was with us.

"Now, Granddaughter, watch and listen deeply, carefully, with all your being."

Grandfather took the bundle of sage from my hand. With a flick of the wrist, he opened his old Zippo lighter and held the sweet-smelling grass over the blue flame. Silver smoke rose in the air. The ceremony had begun.

Grandfather said some words in Lakota and waved the glowing bundle over my shoulders and head. The smoke poured over me like a waterfall. He then did the same thing over his own head. "This is called smudging. The sage purifies us for what we are about to do," he explained. "We must be humble. We must make ourselves smaller than even the tiniest beetle when we go before Wakan Tanka and Mother Earth."

He laid the burning grass down on the spot he'd cleared in the snow. As we crouched beside the wall to keep out of the wind, smoke enveloped us like incense. He gave me a sprig of unburned sage. "Put it behind your ear."

I didn't ask why. I stuck the grass behind my ear like a pencil.

Grandfather tucked some in his hatband. "We wear sage because it's a sign our hearts and minds are close to Wakan Tanka."

Next, he took a braid of the honey-colored sweetgrass and gave it to me.

"Light it," he said as he handed me the ancient lighter he'd had since he was a young sailor. It was rubbed smooth as marble.

I clumsily flicked the flint. Nothing happened.

Grandfather chuckled. He put his thumb over mine and flicked. A tiny, blue flame sprang to life, which he gently cupped in his hands to protect from the wind. "There, now light the grass."

The sweetgrass glowed orange over the flame. Its rich smoke blended with the pungent sage.

"Now wave it in the air."

I did . . . and felt a sense of wonder. My heart began to beat faster.

"The smoke from the sweetgrass will rise up to Wakan Tanka and spread throughout the universe," Grandfather explained quietly. "Its fragrance is known by all that fly, run, creep, swim, or walk. We are all relatives."

After I finished he took the burning sweetgrass and laid it next to the smoldering sage. Then finally he removed the sacred pipe from its case. Its feathers rustled in the wind like whispers. "Hold this, my grand-daughter. Respect its power."

When he passed the pipe to me, the wind cried more fiercely than ever. Grandfather's hat blew off. With trembling hands, I received the pipe. The wind fell quiet as I gripped the pipe, terrified I'd drop it.

Then Grandfather took a large pinch of reddish brown tobacco and held it up to the four directions. He tamped the tobacco down firmly in the pipe bowl. When he finished he looked at me and asked if I had any questions.

I certainly did. "How did you know you were destined to be a medicine man, Grandfather?"

"Someone told me."

"Who?"

"Wanbli Galeshka, the Spotted Eagle. That's from whom I get my name. To our people, he's the Great Spirit's messenger. He appeared to me on my first vision quest."

"When was that?"

"I'd just returned to the reservation from overseas. I needed to get right with Wakan Tanka. For four days and nights I sat on a rocky hilltop, crying for a vision. I had a blanket, a canteen, and no food. On the fourth night a terrible thunderstorm arose. That's when it happened."

My eyes got big. "What happened?"

"Lightning crashed all around me. A white-hot bolt hit a nearby pine tree, and the tree went up like a torch. Wanbli Galeshka rode that thunderbolt, Takoja. I saw him, clear as day. When the sun rose the next morning, an eagle feather rested at my feet. I knew then what I was supposed to do with my life."

"Did it work out like you hoped? Your life and all, I mean."

He looked at me gravely. "The very fact that you are here today makes it so."

I didn't know what to say to a compliment like that. I concentrated on not fumbling the pipe. My hands were sweating. At least they weren't cold any more.

"When he gets old," Grandfather went on, "a medicine man tries to pass on his vision. That's not always easy. It's pretty hard to find the right person. One of the greatest days of my life was when I did."

"How did you find out?"

"Mato hemakiye," he said in Lakota.

"What?"

"Mato hemakiye. It means a bear told me so. In a dream."

I lifted my eyebrows.

"Seriously. I dreamt a big hair Mato knocked on my door one day. As soon as I let him in, he plopped down in front of the fireplace, crossed his legs and asked for a glass of water. Dreams are kind of funny sometimes. Anyway, after I fetched him his drink, he said he'd found somebody for me." Grandfather smiled. "It's you."

The wind howled like a pack of wolves on the hunt. Before I could react Grandfather whispered, "Give me the pipe. It's time."

I couldn't move. He took the pipe from me. In a funny way, I was almost glad to give it back to him. It felt alive.

Grandfather lit the pipe and puffed slowly, stopping four times to let the smoke rise. Each time he puffed the tobacco in the bowl glowed blood red in the darkness. "The smoke of the pipe represents the breath of the Great Spirit, Takoja." He fanned the smoke toward me with the eagle feather from his medicine bundle. "Let your thoughts for Peter rise with the smoke, Granddaughter."

I closed my eyes. When I opened them again, he was standing. He swayed from side to side in the wind.

He shouted to be heard. "Watch me closely, Feather. Someday you'll have to do this. You may not understand everything, but just think about Peter and pray for him to get well. Wakan Tanka will hear and understand."

Grandfather lifted the pipe stem toward the stars. With his long, white hair streaming behind him like a flag, he cried: "Wakan Tanka! Mighty Creator of the Universe, you have always existed, before time, before space, forever and ever! Everything on this earth is yours and calls itself your child. Great Spirit, have mercy on me! Wakan Tanka, please heal my little grandson!"

He touched the pipe to the ground. "Mother Earth, we know it is from your body that our bodies are born! As truly as we know anything, we know we are your sons and daughters. Great Mother, hear my prayers! Please heal my little grandson!"

Then, to each of the four directions, he held the pipe and cried, "Great Mystery of the Universe! Sustainer of the stars and planets, He who is greater than great! Have mercy on me! Please heal my little grandson!"

Silhouetted against the sky, Grandfather then raised the pipe to the heavens one last time. The city lights illuminated the black outline of his figure like a halo. For a few seconds he stood motionless, balanced and perfect. It was like he had stopped time. Then he bowed his head and noiselessly returned to my side.

I gasped when I saw his face. It glowed with a strange inner light, like stained glass in a cathedral. He was beautiful, exhausted and at peace.

"Gather your belongings, Takoja," he said. "We're done. We've been to the mountaintop. Now we go see Peter. The rest belongs to the Creator."

As I scooped up our parcels, the wind wolves hunted in the distance. It was going to be a cold night. I flipped up my collar and wondered what the morning would bring. Whatever it was, I prayed it was good.

Larry, the nice man from the ticket desk, met us at the door. He must've been waiting the whole time we were outside. Opening the door for us, he looked like he wanted something. As it turns out, he did. He wanted to be friends.

"Jeez, you guys look frozen, like a couple of Popsicles. Do you wanna come in the office and warm up? Can I get you a coffee? Maybe a Danish?"

"Thank you so much," said Grandfather warmly, "but we're in a bit of a hurry. We're late for an appointment."

"Late? Oh, no. Gosh, let me show you out anyhow," pleaded Larry. "I mean, it's the least I can do. And, hey, I know a shortcut. I work here, remember." Then he ran over and stuck his head in the office door. "Yvonne," he called, "hold down the fort a second, will you?"

"Will do!" Yvonne yelled back from wherever she was hiding.

Larry guided us past the public elevators. "Forget those, they'll take forever, believe me." He led us through a door and down another hall. I nearly had to trot to keep up. "Here we are," he finally said. "The freight elevator. Nonstop express all the way down. Good luck!"

He pushed the button for us. "By the way, where are you guys headed, if you don't mind me asking?" He held the elevator door open with his elbow. I could tell he was concerned. I think he was embarrassed by the way Yvonne and he acted when they first saw us.

"We need to go to St. Luke's Roosevelt Hospital," said Grandfather. "It's my grandson. He's awfully sick."

Larry frowned. "Uptown? This time of day? You'll never get a cab." He shook his head. "Let me think." Then he snapped his fingers. "Wait! I know what! I'll take you!"

"Please don't go out of your way," protested Grandfather. "You've already been more than kind."

"I insist!" Larry shook his head. "It's the least I can do. I was leaving soon anyway. Your grandson, you say? How could I not?"

Larry was transformed. He was a man with a mission. First he ran back to the office and grabbed his overcoat. Then he took command. "Come on!" he ordered. "We're burning daylight!" He leapt on the elevator like a gazelle.

Once we got downstairs he hurriedly escorted us out to Thirty-Fourth Street.

"Ta-dah! Your chariot awaits!" He stepped aside and gestured to a battered green minivan parked half on, half off the curb. I noticed a ticket under the windshield wiper. The license plate read "Dads Taxi." We got in gratefully.

Somewhere on Eighth Avenue during the ride uptown, Larry turned on the radio, but the volume was deafening. A screeching noise filled the car. Quite frankly, it sounded like someone was squeezing a cat. Larry yanked out the CD. "Oh, Lord! That Miley Cyrus again! Sheesh! I gotta talk to my kids!"

Grandfather and I chuckled.

A short while later when we drove up to the hospital, Larry parked in a loading zone, jumped out, and opened our door for us. "Here you are!" he announced with pride. "Take care. I sure hope the little guy gets better. Marge and the kids and I will say a prayer for him tonight."

Grandfather shook his hand and smiled at him. "You're a good man, my friend. I won't forget what you did for us."

Larry blushed. The top of his bald head turned pink as a boiled lobster.

When he drove off we waved at him until his tail-lights disappeared. As he turned the corner, he hit a pothole and lost a hubcap.

"What a great guy. He really was worthy to touch the pipe," I said. "Wasn't he?"

"Very much so," said Grandfather. He put his arm around me as we entered the hospital. "Now . . . let's go find Peter."

CHAPTER THIRTEEN

inding Peter wasn't so easy. He'd been moved to another floor, and the lady behind the reception desk couldn't pull up his new room on the computer. Her fingers click-clacked over the keyboard. She stared at the paint smeared across Grandfather's face and scowled. "What was that name again?"

"Anderson. Peter Anderson," Grandfather enunciated slowly. He looked tired.

An ambulance screamed outside. Pretty soon an orderly rushed by with a little girl on a gurney. The poor kid had an IV stuck in her arm and oxygen tubes in her nose. Down the hall someone was yelling in Spanish. Overhead the PA crackled, frantically calling doctors to the emergency room.

Apparently Grandfather was going to be at the desk for a while because the computer was down. My friend Emily was probably about to have a stroke. With

Grandfather tied up, now was a good time to call her. I grabbed my cell out of my coat and speed-dialed her number. Nothing happened. My battery was dead. Sighing I went and found the public telephones, but two of them were out of order and the others were busy.

The lady on the phone in line in front of me was crying. Really bawling. Her shoulders bounced up and down with every sob. "I know, Grammie, I know. I'll call you when I find out more," she sniffed. "But, he's okay. Jamal's okay! Bye!"

When she turned around, her faced glowed like an angel. She was crying tears of joy, not sadness. Maybe hospitals aren't so depressing after all. The woman wiped her tears on the sleeve of her coat. I remembered that I had one of those little packages of Kleenex in my coat pocket, so I gave it to her.

"Thank you, darling. Bless you," she gushed, smiling at me with real gratitude as she moved away from the phone. She dried her eyes and flashed me a big smile. I was happy for her.

I searched my change purse for a quarter. Unfortunately all I came up with was four pennies, a wadded dollar bill and a furry lemon Pez. Just my luck. I slammed down the receiver and went to Grandfather. "You don't happen to have twenty-five cents, do you?"

"No, Takoja," he wearily replied. "I spent all my money at the Empire State Building."

I tried the computer lady. "Ma'am? Excuse me, please."

She peered at me over her bifocals. "Yes?" she asked sourly.

"May I have change for a dollar, please?"

"What do I look like, a bank?" she said sarcastically and went right back to messing with the computer.

Great. I took a seat in the waiting area. All around me people slept, ate, or talked; their faces lined with worry. Some looked like they were camping out, like they'd been there for days. I began to feel hot. I remembered all the gear I was wearing, so I took off my hat and scratched my head. It wasn't enough, so I took off my jacket. As I did, I accidentally snagged the necklace Mrs. Green gave me, the one threaded with a pebble and a quarter! I'd just found my change! I slipped the necklace over my head and untied the knot. And the coin fell right in my palm!

I ran to the phones before anyone else could cut in front of me and kissed the quarter for good luck before dropping it in the slot. When I heard the dial tone, I punched in Emily's number.

"Hello?" Oh, it was the voice of Emily's smart-alecky older brother, Yuri.

"Hey, Yuri. This is Feather. What are you doing answering Emily's phone?"

"What do you think, Einstein? She left it lying around again. I found it on the sofa."

While Emily's brother and I usually got along pretty well, right now he was getting on my last nerve. I took a deep breath and tried not to lose my patience. "Is Emily around?"

"No, she's more of a square."

"Yuri, come on, I'm begging you here, I really need to talk to her. Could you put her on?"

"She's not here."

Excellent. And right after she said she'd camp out by the phone until I called. "Where'd she go?"

"To your place, Dumbelina."

"What?"

"She went to see you. At least that's what she told Mom. Wait'll Mom hears this, Em will be so busted!"

"Yuri, please, you can squeal on your sister later. Listen, when did she leave?"

"What's it to ya?"

"Yuri!"

"About twenty minutes ago, if you have to know. Mom was gonna drop her off at your building on her way to a meeting."

Twenty minutes. I'd just missed her.

"Hey! What are you two little twerps up to? Where are you?"

"Never mind," I fumed. On second thought, though, I decided I'd better tell him. "No, actually I'm at St. Luke's Roosevelt Hospital. Emily will understand."

"What?"

"Just tell her I'm at the hospital, please. She knows where. Bye."

I hung up in frustration. I'd wasted my only quarter talking to Yuri, the King of the Wise Guys. I knew he'd give Emily the message, though. He really wasn't such a bad guy, actually. Not the worst, anyway, and not that I'd ever let him know that.

As I walked away from the phone, Mrs. Green's quarter dropped into the coin return with a clink. I had a twenty-five cent boomerang on my hands. I dialed my home number.

"Feather! How good to hear you!"

Mrs. Silverman! Mrs. Silverman is sort of the hall monitor for our building. Actually, she owns the building, and lots of others down in her old neighborhood around Delancey Street where she grew up. Anyway, she loves to visit people all day, roaming from floor to floor, dropping off cakes and pies like some kind of crazed pastry fairy. It's like her entire life now that her husband is gone. She's always using her master key and popping in unannounced with a tray full of goodies. She scares the heck out of me when she does that. Some of the neighbors make fun of her behind her back, but I think she's really sweet. She especially loves to bake Peter and me chocolate chip cookies. And to tell the truth, she really seems to go for Grandfather in a big way.

"Hi, Mrs. Silverman, is—"

"Where are you, sweetie? Your mother is absolutely beside herself. All the calling, I can't begin to tell you . . . not that she should panic, God forbid. I told her you were with Spotted Eagle, so what's to worry? Anyway—"

"Um, Mrs. Silverman, we're at the hospital—"

"I knew it! Your mother's there, too, of course. Such a fine mother to her children, not that she couldn't make more time for you and your darling brother occasionally, but it's not my place to say, right? Go make nice and she'll be eating out of the palm of your—"

I interrupted. Mrs. Silverman is also a champion talker. "Please, is Emily there by any chance? She told her brother she was coming over."

"Emily Feferman? Your little friend? She's right here. Such a nice girl . . ." Mrs. Silverman's voice trailed away. I imagined she was pinching Emily's cheek right about now.

"Such a pretty young lady. The boys . . . the boys don't know what they're in for. Mr. Silverman, God rest his soul, used to say I was quite the one myself, a regular minx."

As much as I adore Mrs. Silverman, I didn't have time for one of her stories. They tend to go on for a while. "Mrs. Silverman, may I speak with her, please?"

"Of course, darling. We're in the kitchen. I just brought over a plate of strawberry blintzes for your grandfather and I'm giving Emily the recipe. She's going to be the next great chef, let me tell you. A regular Wolfgang Hockey Puck. I'll go get her." Mrs. Silverman dropped the phone. In a minute I heard Emily breathing on the other end of the line, obviously waiting for Mrs. Silverman to get out of earshot.

"Emily?"

"Hang on. It's not safe," she whispered dramatically.

"What's she doing there, anyway? I mean, besides transporting blintzes. As a matter of fact, what are you doing there?"

"Your grandfather asked Mrs. Silverman to feed your cat while you guys were gone. Me? I just had to get out of the house. I was going crazy waiting for you to call all afternoon. So I thought I'd meet you when you got home. I brought the key you gave me, but Mrs. Silverman opened the door from inside when she heard me messing with the lock. Man, she scared the heck out of me! Anyway, I just wanted to come over. You know, like a surprise. What in the world is going on?"

"It's a long story. You'll never believe—"

"Omigosh!" Emily suddenly blurted. "Where's my phone? Where are you?"

"Your phone's at home on the sofa where you left it and I'm at St. Luke's. We just got here. But the computer's down and they won't let us up yet. Why?"

"Omigosh! Omigosh! What about the zoo? Omigosh!"

"Emily, please calm down a little—"

"Have you seen your mother? Omigosh, of course you haven't, otherwise—"

"Otherwise, what?" I asked suspiciously.

"Otherwise, you'd know."

"Know what? Emily! What?"

Emily didn't answer.

"Come on, tell me!"

"You better sit down, Feather."

"Okay, okay, I'm sitting down," I lied. "Hurry up and tell me!"

"Well, Peter is really sick, Feather. They think he might . . . might not make it. I'm sorry."

It felt like there was a big hole in my stomach. My worst fears had come true. I sat on the floor because I suddenly felt so heavy, like I was carrying the world's weight on my shoulders.

"Feather? I'm coming down there to be with you. Okay?"

"You . . . you don't have to do that," I said weakly and very unconvincingly.

"I'm coming, Feather. Period!" Emily insisted.

I swallowed hard. "How did you find out about all this?"

"Your dad called a minute ago. He got into town and went straight to the hospital. He called from there. Geez, you haven't even seen any of them yet. Why won't they let you in to see Peter?"

But I had more burning questions to ask. "Wh-what about Mom? Have you heard anymore from her?"

"She's seriously berserk. I think she's afraid you're knocked out in an alley somewhere or something. She called our house twice. I don't know how many times she's called here. Mrs. Silverman said it was a lot."

"Oh." A tidal wave of guilt washed over me. Like Peter being sick wasn't bad enough for her, Mom was worried about me, too. I felt nauseous. I could just hear her calling me "immature" and "irresponsible," telling me that I'd screwed up royally once again.

"Feather, are you still there?"

"Yeah, I'm here." I sighed wearily.

"I'm coming, Feather. Be brave. I'll be there real soon. Somehow I'll get there. Honest."

Before I could stop her, she hung up. I looked over at Grandfather, and suddenly what stood out to me was the dirty cowboy hat he wore, the painted face and rumpled paper bag. He looked like one of those guys you avoid when you see them staggering down Lexington, babbling to themselves.

My conscience started in on me big time. I could just hear Mom. She'd say that while my brother lay dying, I'd wasted the whole day on a wild goose chase with a loony old man. That the two of us were people who saw ghosts, no less, and thought dreams came true. That's exactly what she'd say. And I had to admit—the toy store, Mrs. Chen's, the episode at the zoo, the ceremony at the Empire State Building—when you looked at it from her point of view, it all did seem pretty crazy.

But wait a minute, I thought. That's what she'd say, not me. I looked back at Grandfather, still standing at the hospital desk, and saw a wise old man filled with love for his grandson, who loved his daughter and granddaughter, who was in touch with something mysterious, but which I knew was real. I'd been there with him. And I knew this was where I was supposed to be. I dropped the telephone into its cradle. Mrs. Green's boomerang quarter fell into the change slot with a "clink." I went over to Grandfather and put my arms around his neck.

"Grandfather, did you find out where Peter is?"

"He's in room 816. It took a while to find the new room number because the paperwork wasn't done, but Mrs. Grabowski here was very resourceful."

"All right!" I erupted with real emotion.

For the first time she smiled. "I hope your brother feels better," she said, genuinely concerned.

"He will," I assured her. "I'm sure of it!"

But by the time Grandfather and I stood in front of Peter's door, I wasn't sure of anything. Somewhere between the reception desk and the eighth floor, my confidence had dissolved. I couldn't believe how anxious I felt. Grandfather and I looked at each other, took a deep breath, and then knocked on the door.

"Come in." It was my mother's voice.

Grandfather went in. I took another deep breath and followed. The room was dark and the air seemed filled with fear. Half hidden by a curtain, a doctor and a nurse huddled over the bed. I couldn't see Peter. Mom's camel hair coat was on the floor and a bunch of hamburger wrappers was stuffed in the trashcan. I could smell a greasy French fry smell, and I spotted at least three empty Diet Coke cans.

Mom bolted past Grandfather without a word. She looked awful. Her hair looked a mess and deep purple bags rimmed her eyes. I noticed she had on the same outfit she'd worn to the office the day before, which was not like her at all.

"Where on earth have you been?" she roared at me when she saw us enter. "You better have a good explanation, young lady! Why didn't you take my calls? I was worried sick! How could you be so selfish?"

All the blood drained out of my head. I was speechless.

Ignoring me, she then turned on Grandfather. She glared daggers at the sacred pipe. "I'm sure this was all your doing!"

Grandfather slowly nodded. "Yes, like you say, it was all my doing."

"I should have known," Mom said. "Oh, Pop, I just don't know what to do with—" Her voice trailed off. She crossed her arms and then peered closer, finally noticing Grandfather's paint. "What is all that mess on your face?" she said, clearly horrified.

"It doesn't matter, Ann. All that counts is that they're here," someone said from the shadows. Dad! He rose from a swivel chair on the far side of the bed. I hadn't seen him in months. His hair was a lot longer and he'd grown a reddish-brown beard. Plus he was really tan. He still wore the familiar tweed jacket with the leather elbow patches and round, steel-rimmed glasses, though. "Are you all right, honey?" he asked in his soothing, loving voice.

Tears filling my eyes, I shook my head up and down while we hugged each other a very long time.

Suddenly another nurse came in, and Mom went over and whispered to the doctor. I guess she was through interrogating us for the time being.

Dad shook hands with Grandfather. "It's good to see you, Spotted Eagle."

"And good to see you, Will," Grandfather answered. He liked Dad despite all the mean things Mom said about him during the divorce proceedings—some of which were true.

While they talked, I approached the foot of Peter's bed. That's when I noticed Mr. Houghton, the head of Mom's law firm. I wondered why he was lurking around. He didn't seem like the kind of person who would visit a sick kid he didn't know. Then it hit me. I bet that he wanted to date Mom. Maybe he already had. I ignored him. One of the nurses was busy taking Peter's blood pressure. When she moved out of the way to pull the curtain back a little, I wasn't ready for what I saw.

Peter was scrunched up in a ball. An oxygen mask covered most of his face. His eyes were closed and his forehead was pale and drenched with sweat. In the middle of that big bed he looked like a tiny, broken doll. But he wasn't alone. Max, his faithful teddy, lay on the pillow next to him.

Grandfather came and stood by me.

"I wish I could do something to help him," I whispered to him.

"You already have, Takoja. You've been to the mountaintop. Now you must be strong for him. He needs you."

"You'll have to move, please," said the doctor, as she placed her stethoscope on Peter's chest.

A busty blonde nurse took me by the elbow. "Come on, you can watch cartoons in the lounge. It'll be fun," she crooned in that babyish tone of voice that adults use when they want you to do something you'd rather not.

"No!" I protested. "He needs me!" I kissed Peter on the forehead then tucked in White Buffalo Calf Girl beside him under the sheets.

"Do what she says this instant!" ordered Mom.

"Hang on a minute, Ann. She's not hurting anything. She's just trying to help, that's all," said Dad, rising to my defense.

"Don't start with me, Bill!" Mom said. "You can't begin acting like a concerned parent this late in the game." Her eyes were filled with hatred.

Creepy Mr. Houghton put his hand on the collar of my jacket. "Come along, young lady, this is no place for a child," he said crisply, pulling me toward the door. I think maybe he was trying to impress Mom.

"She's not a child, and she's staying!" Everyone gaped at Grandfather. "Take your hands off her," he growled. "Now!"

Mr. Houghton looked like he'd been slapped in the face. He let go of me and started nervously picking lint off his Armani suit coat.

Somebody tapped on the door, and Dad sprang to open it. There stood Emily, holding a big bouquet of flowers in her right hand. Perfect timing! She grinned sheepishly and took a step forward. "Am I interrupting anything?"

CHAPTER FOURTEEN

"That's it! I can't treat this patient if you people insist on turning this place into a circus! Everybody out now—except for the immediate family!" the doctor roared, red in the face.

"Wait," Dad pleaded. "It's all right. She's like family." He took Emily's flowers and said warmly, "Come on in, Emily. These are lovely roses. Thank you."

"Uh, I can leave if this isn't a good time," Emily whispered, seeing the expression on Mom's face, and backed away. I think she would've kept going until she hit Connecticut if she hadn't bumped into Mrs. Silverman and the large Tupperware bowl she was carrying.

Mrs. Silverman cheerfully propelled Emily back into the room. "Don't be shy, darling. Don't be shy," she said, as she gave the container to one of the nurses.

"Refrigerate this, darling. A cup when he wakes up is fine. And be sure you heat it up in the microwave, beforehand."

"Wh-what is this?" blurted the astounded nurse.

"Soup. Don't thank me," Mrs. Silverman beamed. "My special recipe. I swear to you, Rabbi Hirsch is alive today because of it."

"I can't believe this," groaned the doctor, smacking her forehead.

"Hello, Sylvia. How thoughtful of you to come," said Grandfather warmly.

Mrs. Silverman pinched his cheek. "What a mensch. You, I'll get to later. Where's my boy?" On her way to see Peter, she collided with Mr. Houghton, who grimaced in distaste.

"I don't believe I've had the pleasure," he mouthed off snidely.

"You should be so lucky," smirked Mrs. Silverman, seeing right through him. She peeled off her fake fur overcoat and gave it to him like he was a servant, knowing it would rile him. "Don't worry, no claim ticket is necessary. I trust you."

"Why, I've never!" he huffed. He threw the coat on a nearby stool and stormed from the room as Mom ran after him.

At that point the doctor slapped Peter's chart down on the bedside table. "That does it! Everybody out! Family included!"

Emily jumped and pushed me into the hall, as Mrs. Silverman paused in the doorway. "The poor doctor is obviously overworked," she said, looking back at my mother. "She's so tired she doesn't know what she's saying. Why don't you two get yourselves a nice soda? By the time you get back, I'll have her eating out of the palm of my hand." She smiled her patented Mrs. Silverman smile and shut the door with a click. It was obvious the adults were staying.

Emily threw her arm around my shoulders and moved me along with her. "So what's going on? How is Peter? Any change?"

I looked down at the floor. "No."

She squeezed my hand and gently bumped her head against mine. "Cheer up! He'll be okay. I just know it."

"Thanks for coming, Emily."

"Forget about it. That's what friends are for," she said, trying to cheer me up.

"You guys got here pretty quick," I said.

Emily grabbed my wrist. "Omigosh, I haven't told you, have I? You are absolutely not going to believe this!"

"What?"

"Okay, like it was, what, 6:30 maybe when you called? Okay, so Mrs. Silverman grabs the soup off the stove, feeds Miko some Tender Vittles and we go downstairs, right? Like in a big hurry and all."

"Yeah, I can see that," I chuckled. Emily enjoys being in a big hurry. It makes things more dramatic. And she was definitely "on" today. Her perm bounced like a Jeep with bad shocks.

"Well, I'm freaking, because like there's probably no way we're going to get a cab this time of night, you know. I'm a native New Yorker, I'm on to these things, right?"

I nodded. "Right."

"So guess what happened."

"You got a cab."

Emily frowned. "How did you know?"

"Lucky guess. You got here so fast and all."

"Well, you'll never guess the next part."

I lifted my eyebrows.

"I'm totally and completely serious here, Feather!"

I cooperated. "You got me. Go on."

"As soon as we set foot outside the building, we get a cab."

"No way."

"Way. Very way. I mean, who would believe it? While I'm towing Mrs. Silverman, who also, I might remind you, is lugging this totally embarrassing king-sized tub of chicken soup, a cab pulls over. Out of the blue. I hadn't even hailed it yet. Go figure."

"Amazing."

"Wait, it gets better. Okay, so we jump in the taxi, in a big hurry and all, and guess what?"

"What?"

"We land right on top of this . . . this person!" She paused for effect.

I took my cue. "Who?"

"A little old Chinese lady. She was the cutest thing. I mean, her wrinkles had wrinkles."

My heart skipped a beat. Mrs. Chen! It had to be her.

"Feather, are you okay? You look sort of dazed."

"Yes . . . no . . . I mean . . . I'm fine," I said. "Could you, uh, repeat that last part?"

"You betcha," nodded Emily. Actually, she adores repeating her stories, and they only get better with time. She took a deep breath. "As I said Mrs. S. and I hop in the cab with this crazy little Chinese lady. I mean, she was wearing red tennies of all things. She was really sweet. Anyway—"

"You didn't happen to catch her name, did you?"

Emily looked puzzled. "Now that you mention it, no. But, anyway, right off the bat, she's like our best friend. She says she saw us on the sidewalk and we looked like we needed a ride. She says she told the cabbie to pull right over. Can you believe it? Then she hands me the bouquet. And get this. She said it might come in handy where we were going. Go figure, again."

"Yeah, go figure," I replied, only half listening.

"Well, hang on, I haven't told you the strangest part."

"Which is?"

Emily paused for maximum effect, and then whispered, "The cabbie was a—"

I knew what she was about to say. The hair on the back of my neck crinkled.

"—Native American."

Call me psychic. Mrs. Chen and the Indian cabbie ... together. I remembered what Grandfather said about everything being connected.

"This guy was kind of a younger version of your grandpa. And ... and ... hey, Feather." Emily waved her hand in front of my face and snapped her fingers. "Feather?"

"Wh-what?" I blinked.

"Are you sure you're all right?"

"Yeah, sure, I'm fine," I forced myself to say. "I'm just a little warm."

Emily went to the water cooler across the hall and brought back a paper cup full of cold water. "Drink this. You don't look so perky."

I gulped the water. "Thanks. You take good care of me, Emily."

"Anyway . . ." Emily took a deep breath. "Anyway, I saved the best for last. I haven't told you the most bizarre part."

"You didn't see the cab drive away, did you? It just sort of vanished . . . right?"

She gawked at me like I'd just told her I was from Venus and needed her brain for an experiment. "H-How did you know?"

"It's another long story. Trust me," I answered.

"But, but—"

"Trust me."

Just then a commotion erupted inside the room. All this time we were still in the hallway. But even with the door closed, I could hear it. There was no way I was staying out now. I barged in, dragging Emily behind me.

"He wants to do what?" blared the red-faced doctor.

"It's a prayer, basically," Dad explained, "an age-old ceremonial recognition of the powers of—"

The doctor pushed up the sleeves of her white coat, crossed her arms and exploded: "Absolutely not! I won't permit it! Under any circumstances! For God's sake, we're in a hospital. This child is on oxygen. Do you want to start a fire?"

One of the nurses shot past me. She looked real scared. I heard her rubber-soled shoes squeaking on the linoleum as she ran down the hall.

Then Mrs. Silverman sidled over to the doctor, smiling coyly at her, her eyes twinkling, really laying it on with a trowel. Trust me, it was worth the price of admission just to watch her work. "What's with all the kvetching?" she shrugged. "Is a teensy-weensy ceremony so bad? Leave the room, why don't you? Who'll know?"

I tugged the tail of Dad's jacket. "What's going on?"

"Spotted Eagle wants to pray for Peter with that pipe he's carrying," he explained. "And maybe burn some sweetgrass. It's a kind of special plant. I know you probably won't understand, but it's all part of an ancient shamanic ritual."

I humored Dad. "Gee," I whispered, "an ancient ritual. What'll they think of next?"

Ever the anthropologist Dad stroked his beard as he narrated the scene before us. "The good doctor here is coming from a different frame of cultural reference. Basically she doesn't think a pipe ceremony is a wise idea."

"I can tell," I said. "But she's wrong."

Grandfather cleared his throat. His face was grave. His words came slowly. "I am an old man. I only know a few things. When I was younger, well, I knew many things. Many. Now, I am not so certain. Most of life is a great mystery to me." He bowed his head. "And that is as it should be. I've learned there is a big difference between knowledge and wisdom."

The doctor cut in. "Well, frankly, I don't see what—"

Grandfather silenced her with the steely look of an eagle. He slipped the pipecase off his shoulder. When the other nurse saw this, she said, "I'll get security!" and made a break for it like the other one who shot past us when we came in.

Grandfather unsheathed the pipe, and the doctor took a step back.

Dad gave a low whistle and exclaimed, "My Lord, in all my years of research, I've never seen such a remarkable specimen."

As he extended his hands toward the pipe, Mrs. Silverman grabbed his wrist. "Specimen, schmecimen. Ask for permission like a nice boy," she said. She knew she was in the presence of something very special. I could see it in her face. It glowed.

"The sacred pipe links us to all living things, even unto the earth and sky," Grandfather said, never taking his eyes off the doctor. "For thousands of years my people have put their trust in it. Though we have suffered much, the pipe has never forsaken us."

The doctor shook her head. "Certainly, you're not suggesting—"

Grandfather talked over her protests. "I love that little boy lying there more than anything in this world. I will do whatever is in my power to help him. We've tried your way of pills and machines. All I ask is that you let me try mine—the way of my ancestors and his. He is half Lakota, you know."

With a sigh the doctor replied, "Sir, I respect your colorful, shall we say, opinions, but I really don't have time for a lecture on—"

I had heard enough. I had really lost my patience by now. Suddenly I found my voice. "Just because you can't imagine something doesn't mean it's not real. Anybody knows that!"

The doctor stared at me in disbelief. Her cheek twitched. Then she pretended to ignore me, like I wasn't worth her valuable adult time.

Looking down her nose at Grandfather, she grunted, "However limited my imagination, and however allegedly noble your motivations may be, sir, I still cannot allow you to interfere with the safe and proper operation of this institution. Furthermore—"

Suddenly, the door flew open with a bang. I nearly jumped through the roof.

CHAPTER FIFTEEN

"What in God's name is going on in here?" Mom demanded to know. "A nurse claims you're all trying to torch the place."

Nobody said anything.

She fastened her gaze on Grandfather. "Well?" Her sarcastic tone of voice was all too familiar. I cringed and looked at Grandfather. He stood stock still and didn't say anything. It was as though he was no longer there for her. His whole being seemed riveted solely on Peter.

The doctor stepped forward. "Ms. Anderson, your father unfortunately insists on conducting some sort of primitive rite which I simply cannot countenance at all, seeing as to how—"

"That's not true!" I protested. "You still don't understand! None of you do! He only wants to pray for Peter!"

Just then the nurse called the doctor out of the room.

Mom narrowed her eyes at me. "That's enough, missy. I'll deal with you later!"

Dad tried to defend me. "Ann, don't be so upset. This isn't what it looks like. All Spotted Eagle wants is—"

Mom cut him off at the knees. "I know what it looks like, Bill. It looks like a superstitious old man is being encouraged by two kids, an incredibly immature adult who ought to know better, and the neighborhood gossip."

"Gossip?" Mrs. Silverman gasped, obviously hurt.

Grandfather's face clouded with concern. He was back in our reality now, I guess you could say. "There's no need for such hot words, Ann. I know how anxious you are about Peter, but you shouldn't take out your fear on people who only want to help. Direct your anger at me."

"Come on, Dad. Outside. I don't have time for this!" Mom snapped, speaking to him like he was a little kid. Her public show of disrespect for Grandfather killed me. The fact that she did it in front of strangers made it even worse.

Grandfather didn't move. "Do you truly feel nothing for the ways of your people, my daughter? Are their campfires turned to ashes in your heart?"

Mom closed her eyes and ran her fingers through her hair. Her jaw muscles clenched. Suddenly she seized him by the arm and started to lead him away. "Dad, I really, really don't have time for this. Come on."

He pulled free. "No. My place is with my grandson. He deserves the prayers of his people. He is a Lakota. And so are you . . . if you haven't forgotten."

Mom lost it. "You don't get it, Dad! He's in a coma!" She went to Peter's bed. "Look at him!" She lifted the sheet. "Look at him! There's absolutely nothing you can do! For God's sake, don't be a fool. Be realistic for once in your life!" Her chin trembled and tears rimmed her eyes.

"Ann, that's completely uncalled for," Dad protested, veins bulging in his neck.

Grandfather managed to keep his cool. "Children, please. Don't fight." He rested his hand on Mom's shoulder. "Help me. Help me with the pipe. Listen to the ancestral wisdom that is in your blood. Come with me and walk the old path again. For Peter's sake . . . and yours."

Hot tears glistened in Mom's eyes. She twisted her face away and groaned, "Oh, Dad, you live in a dream world. It's not that easy. I can never go back. Never."

The doctor returned and said quietly, "For the sake of the patient, I'm going to have to ask everyone to leave the room. The adult family members may briefly visit but only after we do some more blood work on the patient. Personally I think the children should go home."

That did it. I started crying in anger. "For the sake of the patient? For the sake of the patient? You don't know what to do for the sake of the patient!"

Mom wheeled on me. "That does it, young lady! I've had it up to here with your sullen behavior! You're insolent, childish, and now you're also grounded!"

Grandfather stepped between us like a referee. He gently took me by the elbow. "Come, Takoja. We've done everything we can. We can't do any better than that." He led me toward the door. All I could do was bawl and go along with him. As he passed Mom, he quietly said, "I expected more from you. Maybe I expected too much."

We left the room with Emily and Mrs. Silverman in tow. As she went out the door, Mrs. Silverman got in her two cents worth. "You, a mother! You should be ashamed. Ashamed, I tell you."

In the TV lounge, I collapsed in a chair and sobbed like a baby. It was a real scene. Grandfather, Emily, and Mrs. Silverman clustered around me, patting me and massaging my shoulders. During the whole episode, I hated myself for crying in front of Mom and the doctor. It was like they'd won. But eventually I calmed down. I realized having a fit might make me feel a whole lot better, only it sure wasn't going to help Peter any. To do that, I needed to figure out a plan. I had to be rational. Even better, I had to be clever

. . . real clever. I had to come up with something. So while Emily watched an old *I Love Lucy* rerun, I schemed.

Across the room Grandfather sat talking with Mrs. Silverman, as they drank from two cans of Sprite. Mom and Dad were downstairs handling a foul-up with some insurance paperwork. Unfortunately Mr. Houghton was still lurking around, because Mom told him to make sure Grandfather and I didn't try to go back to Peter's room. He was flipping through an old *New Yorker* as he periodically gave us the evil eye.

After the *Lucy* show was over, I stood up and stretched. I was restless and still hadn't come up with anything. I needed to pace around.

"Pssst, where are you going?" asked Emily, who was being really protective since the scene in the room.

"Oh, nowhere. I just need to visit with Grandfather a second."

"Be my guest." She picked up a *People* magazine. "Ooh! Another article about Brangelina!"

I sat next to Grandfather. "Hi."

Mrs. Silverman blasted out of her chair. "Don't even try to stop me. I won't hear it. You two want to be alone." Then she got up and sat right next to Mr. Houghton. It looked to me like she just wanted to annoy him.

"She's nice, isn't she," I said to Grandfather.

"She's more than nice," he smiled at me. "She's a warrior. You can't imagine what she lived through when she was a teenager in Poland during the war. Some day in school you'll learn about something called the Warsaw Ghetto. Then you'll know. " He was quiet for a moment and then cleared his throat and asked, "By the way, my granddaughter, how are you doing?"

"The big question is how are *you* doing? We've had a long day."

He grunted. "I'm a tough old tatanka buffalo bull. I'm fine." He looked me straight in the eye. I could tell he was about to say something serious. He thought for a moment and said, "Don't blame your mother, Feather, she—"

"She what?" I asked. I was really mad at her.

"She's under a lot of pressure. She has many things on her mind. Peter, the divorce, the office . . . you know how hard she works. And she worries about you, especially you."

"Me?"

"Yes, you. She worries about you not having a father at home. She worries about your schoolwork, what career you'll have when you grow up, things like that. She loves you more than anything, you know."

"Well, I miss Dad and all, but she shouldn't worry about that. I have you. As for a career, I've already decided

I'm going to be a science-fiction writer, or a veterinarian. Maybe I'll be a veterinarian who writes books."

He laughed. "That's good. You'll make a great writer. You'll make a good whatever you want to be. Of that, I'm sure." Then he got all serious again. "You know, your mother worries about me, too. I'm a lot of responsibility. For example I get in the way—"

"That's not true!" I said. I didn't want him to start talking about how old he is. I changed the subject. "I wish we could still do something to help Peter."

"Granddaughter, listen to me. Simply be there for him in your thoughts. Give your burden to Wakan Tanka and Mother Earth. In the end, they are really the only ones who can heal him. We can't. We can only petition them for help."

"What do you mean?"

"We ask them to answer our prayers. Sometimes they do, if we are worthy enough."

"Tunkashila, if they hadn't kicked us out of the room, what were you going to do?"

"I had a traditional healing ceremony in mind. Our people have used it for hundreds of years. It's very powerful, very sacred . . . very Wakan . . . very holy."

"What exactly do you . . . I mean, how does it work?"

"No one knows how it works. That part's a great mystery. But what I do is simple. Mainly I pray with the pipe. First, I purify the tipi, or wherever I am, with sweetgrass, and then I pray and sing healing songs over the person who is ill."

"That's all?"

"Well, there's one more thing. I sprinkle water on them with my medicine feather. You'd be surprised how often patients are cured in this manner."

"Your medicine feather?"

"Yes, my eagle feather. You know, the one I found on the mountain during my first vision quest. Here, I'll show it to you." He unbuttoned his coat and pulled out his medicine bag.

I caught Mr. Houghton watching us closely and frowning. I stuck out my tongue at him. He just shook his head and buried himself back in his magazine.

Grandfather handed me the feather. Most of it was yellowed with age, but the tip was still jet-black. A thin red ribbon was tied to the end.

Suddenly, I shot straight up in my chair. "Grandfather, may I borrow this a minute?"

He didn't hesitate. "Of course, Takoja. But be careful. It's strong medicine."

I tucked the feather under my shirt. I had an idea. It was a long shot, but it just might work . . . if I was worthy enough.

Frank McMillan

Emily's eyes were as big as dinner plates. "You want me to do what?"

"Pipe down, for one thing. Not so loud!" I looked over my shoulder to see what Mr. Houghton was doing. "Create a diversion. I need you to create a diversion."

"Omigosh! Omigosh!"

"Sssh!" I hissed. "Emily, for crying out loud, settle the heck down. You're going to give yourself an embolism."

"A what?"

"Never mind. We need Mrs. Silverman to help us, too, if this is going to work. It's pretty risky."

"Omi-mummph." Emily clamped her hand over her mouth and then took three deep breaths. I think it's a trick her therapist taught her. "What are we going to do?"

"Sneak into Peter's room."

Emily opened her mouth.

"Don't say it," I cautioned.

She shut her mouth.

"Good. Now, let's tell Mrs. Silverman before Mom gets back."

Mrs. Silverman sat, doing her needlepoint in front of the television set. I coughed and she looked up at me and smiled. "Girls, sit down. Tell me some lies."

I sat next to her, but Emily only stared at her like a zombie. "Sit down!" I growled out of the side of my mouth.

Emily blinked and mumbled, "Oh, yeah," as she crash landed into her seat.

Dropping her needle and thread in her lap, Mrs. Silverman twisted her head like a parakeet. "What gives? I can tell you two are plotting. Which I highly approve of, I might add." She smiled encouragingly and waited for my response. She had me cold and she knew it.

I leaned toward her, and whispered, "Okay, here's the plan . . ."

CHAPTER SIXTEEN

*T*en minutes later, we broke the huddle. It was show time. We only had one chance to get things right. I didn't want to think about what would happen if we screwed up. "All right, Em, you know your assignment?"

Emily saluted. "Affirmative! Create a diversion to keep Mr. Houghton off your back." She smiled like a cat that had just devoured several canaries. I could tell her natural love of secrecy had overcome her equally natural fear of . . . of everything. In fact she was downright cocky.

"And you're going to create a diversion by . . . ?"

"That's for me to know and for you to find out," she said playfully. "You mentioned Mr. Houghton is a lawyer, didn't you?"

I squinted at her. "Yeah. He's in Mom's firm. Why?"

"Good. That's all I need to know. Never mind why. If it's a diversion you want, it's a diversion you'll get."

I couldn't imagine what she was cooking up, but I knew I could count on her. I faced Mrs. Silverman. "Are you ready?"

"I was born ready, pardner," Mrs. Silverman drawled in her very best "Lower East Side meets the Wild West" accent. The light of battle gleamed in her eyes. Grandfather was right. The woman was absolutely and totally fearless.

I puffed out my cheeks and blew. "It's now or never. Let's go!"

According to plan, we staggered our takeoff so as not to arouse suspicion. Luckily, Mr. Houghton was buried behind the *New York Times*. Mrs. Silverman got up first and casually walked over to Grandfather, whispering something in his ear. He nodded, but didn't say anything. As Emily and I watched, Mrs. Silverman patted his hand and then went and stood right in the middle of the lounge. Now came the acting.

"Oy!" she exclaimed. "What was I thinking, drinking all that soda? It's going straight through me!"

Some little kids playing on the floor giggled. Mr. Houghton slowly lowered his paper. He glared at Mrs. Silverman, wrinkling his nose in disgust.

She shrugged and smiled at him. "It's rough getting old." Then she held the empty can of Sprite upside down.

Emily took her cue and jumped out of her chair. "I'm due for a bathroom trip, too. I'll go with you, Mrs.

S." She hollered at Mr. Houghton: "Hey, Warden, can we go to the can?"

Mr. Houghton popped his paper and scowled in exasperation. When he managed to sarcastically spit out his permission— "By all means, be my guest," — Emily and Mrs. Silverman exited stage left.

I was alone now. I didn't dare look at Grandfather. I was afraid if I did, I wouldn't go through with my plan. But he was like a magnet. I couldn't help looking at him. There he was with his medicine pipe resting across his knees, calm as could be. He felt my eyes on him and turned to look back at me and then winked. He knew! Mrs. Silverman must've told him our plan when she whispered in his ear. I didn't feel so alone anymore. Silently I mouthed the words, "I love you."

Grandfather answered back with his eyes. "I know. I love you, too."

All of a sudden, I felt like I could take on the world. But I had to wait for our plan to be set in motion. I checked my watch. Emily and Mrs. Silverman had been gone for over five minutes. I couldn't imagine what was keeping them. It was hard, but I stayed put. Mr. Houghton kept reading. Grandfather appeared to be dozing.

After a few more minutes crawled by, I began to worry. What if something had happened to Emily and

Mrs. Silverman? Had they run into the doctor? What if Mom returned before Emily sprang her trap? Images of a thousand different disasters, each more chilling than the one before, paraded through my mind. I had to act soon or I was going to go nuts. Then . . .

"You wanna play?"

An angelic little boy sat next to me who couldn't have been a day over five. He had a death grip on a battered Hot Wheels dragster, obviously a prized possession. Its paint was all rubbed off and a tire was missing.

"Sure, I'll play," I chuckled, grateful for the distraction. "What's your name?"

He wiped his runny nose on the sleeve of his Elmo sweatshirt. "Ahmad."

"Hi, Ahmad. I'm Feather."

Ahmad looked at me out of the corners of his big, brown eyes. "Feather? That's a funny name."

I laughed. "You're right about that. What do you want to play?"

He looked at me like he couldn't believe I'd asked such a stupid question. "Race cars!" he shouted gleefully. "Come on!"

"Where do you think you're going, hmm?" purred Mr. Houghton as I stood up.

Ahmad made a face. "Is that your daddy?"

"Not a chance," I winced, frowning at Mr. Houghton. "Nowhere," I said to the creep. "I'm not going anywhere . . ." I muttered under my breath, ". . . yet."

He rose halfway from his seat. "I didn't catch that!" he snapped. "What was that last smart-alecky remark, young lady?"

"Nothing," I answered in an exaggerated and dramatically meek voice. It went against all my instincts to back down and play the wimp, but I couldn't jeopardize the mission.

"That's better," he said, convinced that he'd put me in my place. When he glanced back to his paper, I stuck out my tongue.

"You're naughty," observed Ahmad.

"I know," I said, "particularly to those who deserve it."

While Ahmad and I played cars, I was beside myself waiting for Emily. Where in the world was she? But I needn't have worried because it didn't take long to find out.

"Help! Omigosh! Help! Help!

I'd know that "Omigosh!" anywhere. It was Emily, screaming for dear life somewhere in the corridor. She was really hamming it up. "Help! Help! Help! I fell and I can't get up! Oh, the pain, the agony! My back! I need legal representation! I'm gonna sue!"

I pinched my nostrils together so I wouldn't laugh.

At the word "sue," Mr. Houghton's ears pricked up like a schnauzer's. Flinging his newspaper aside, he bolted from his chair like a circus clown shot out of a cannon. "Wait! I'm an attorney!" he shouted. Fumbling frantically he snatched a business card from his wallet and hustled from the lounge.

Emily had come through brilliantly. This was the chance I was waiting for. I bounced up off the floor and bolted like a shot for my brother's room.

"Hey! Hang on!" called Ahmad. "We not through with our race! There's still three laps to go!"

In a flash I rounded the last corner before Peter's room. Suddenly someone grabbed me from behind. "What the—" was all I could manage before a hand covered my mouth. Whoever did it was strong as an ox, I thought, while being jerked through a nearby door.

"What took you so long? I was getting more gray hairs already!" smirked a familiar voice. Mrs. Silverman!

When she switched on the light, I realized we were in the laundry room. I turned around and there she was, dressed head to toe in a lime green hospital scrub suit, mask, and matching hat. I was stunned. "Mrs. S-Silverman, what are you doing in here!"

She laughed. "How do you like my outfit? Actually if you want to know the truth, I think it makes my eyes look most attractive." She held a finger to her mask. "Sssh! Now, listen to me. You can't be running around like a bull in a china whatchamacallit with that meshuga doctor lurking in the hallway. We've got to outsmart them all. Here's how we're going to do it." She held out her hand. "Voilà!" She pointed at a gurney piled with rumpled sheets.

"I don't get it."

She put her hands on her hips. "What's not to get? Crawl under the sheets and I'll whisk you straight to Peter's room. If we run into anybody, God forbid, I'll say I'm there to collect the dirty linen. Who can argue? What? They want the little children to have dirty sheets? Of course not! Once we're inside, out you crawl and, bingo, you're in business. You can start the ceremony! What could be simpler?"

I had to admit it was a great plan. "I'm game," I said.

"Of course you are, darling." She pinched my cheek.

I climbed on the gurney and Mrs. Silverman fluffed the sheets over me. They were toasty, fresh out of the dryer, and had that nice, clean smell. We banged through the door.

As we rolled down the hall, I prayed I didn't fall off. The gurney wobbled worse than a grocery cart. It was like sitting on top of a washing machine. "Slow down!" I whispered.

Mrs. Silverman slapped the laundry. "Shush!"

Buried under the sheets, I couldn't see, but at least I could hear. Overhead the intercom droned out an endless list of doctor's names being paged. We passed some visitors talking. A pair of shoes squeaked by us— probably a nurse. Mrs. Silverman said "hello" and kept right on going. So far, so good.

"Excuse me. May I have a blanket?"

Uh oh. I didn't like the sound of that.

Refusing to break stride, Mrs. Silverman played deaf.

"Excuuse me! Bring that bedding back here! I need a change in room 811 on the double!" called another voice. Then a pair of shoes squeaked after us.

Mrs. Silverman slowed to a halt. "Rats!" she muttered under her breath.

"Are you hard of hearing?" asked the voice. Whoever it was, was right next to me. I held my breath.

"Hey, wait a minute! Just a minute, please!" the voice exclaimed with alarm. "I don't recognize you! Who are you? How long have you been working on this floor?"

Mrs. Silverman's tone raised a notch. "Not very long at all, dearie, believe me. Here, have a nice sheet."

"Look, I don't recall ever seeing you before!" the voice didn't give up.

"Bad luck for you then, dearie," Mrs. Silverman laughed nervously.

"You don't get it. I said I don't recognize you, and I'm the supervisor for this ward. Let me see your hospital identification badge."

Mrs. Silverman didn't utter a peep. I closed my eyes. We were as good as dead. But Mrs. Silverman still had one trick up her sleeve. She pretended to cry. I forgot she was a real professional, and a living legend at neighborhood funerals.

"I knew this would happen! The first day on the job for a poor, old woman, and already with the prejudice! My poor Irving!" She sniffed and then took a tissue out of her pocket and blew her nose with a lot of exaggeration.

This time she was laying it on a bit thick, if you ask me. If anything, she was attracting attention.

"And his hernia operation, they won't pay for! Those heartless insurance people! What are they? Made of stone? And me, a poor immigrant!" She blew her nose again. This time it was even louder.

It worked. The charge nurse tried to calm her down. "Look, all I wanted was a blanket, I'm sorry—"

Mrs. Silverman had gone full-steam ahead. She wasn't about to quit. "And the paperwork! Working my fingers to the bone to save my poor Irving, and they won't make with the papers at this miserable, slave-driving hospital fast enough. God forbid you should live to be my age and have to—"

The nurse surrendered without a fight. "Okay, I'm sorry. Forget about it. I'm sorry I bothered you. Really. You poor thing, if they don't get your insurance forms out tomorrow, you tell me, okay?"

Mrs. Silverman honked like a diesel truck and blew her nose. "Oh, thank you, thank you. God bless you," she sobbed.

"And I hope your husband gets better."

"From your mouth to God's ears. Give me a hug, sweetie."

Give me a hug! I gritted my teeth.

When I heard the supervisor's shoes squeak back down the hall, I whispered, "Good job!"

"Right," chuckled Mrs. Silverman, clearly enjoying herself. "I'm a regular Meryl Streep if I do say so myself."

A few more wobbles and we were at Peter's door. Mrs. Silverman pulled the sheets off me and down I hopped as she gave me a big hug. "Hurry, my darling, hurry. Your grandfather is so proud of you!"

"So he knows what I'm doing?"

"He knows and he approves! He said it was all up to you now." She kissed me on both cheeks. "Do what you have to do, angel!" She couldn't resist one last hug. "Such a good girl! God Bless!"

CHAPTER SEVENTEEN

I slipped inside the dimly lit room and hid in the shadows behind the door, as Mrs. Silverman rattled away with the gurney. When she was gone, I tiptoed to Peter's bedside. Barely, just barely, I could hear him breathing. I watched him for a minute while the oxygen flowing into his mask hissed like a faraway river. Then I kissed him on the forehead. He was so hot and damp and pale that it scared me. I reached under the sheets to hold his tiny, limp hand and I cried.

Someone coughed outside in the hall. I knew I didn't have much time. I rubbed away my tears and pressed his fingers to my face. Leaning close to his ear, I whispered, "I love you, Petey. I love you forever." I said it over and over, hoping that somehow he could hear me.

More voices could be heard in the corridor outside. I stood still and listened, but fortunately they went away.

My hands shook. "You've got to hurry, Feather," I said to myself. But I didn't know where to begin.

I pulled Grandfather's sacred eagle feather from under my shirt. The smell of sage and prairies and blue sky filled the air like incense. There was a chance, but was I worthy enough? That was the question. I realized it wasn't up to me to decide and I felt better.

In the healing ceremony, I recalled Grandfather saying he sprinkled the patient with water. I went to the sink and ran the thickest stream of water I dared. Any sound might give me away. Then I twirled the feather in my hand. It somehow didn't seem right to dunk it under the faucet. So I got a paper cup, filled it halfway and dipped the tip of the feather until it was soaked.

I went back to Peter. I thought about how much I loved him until I felt filled with love to the point of overflowing. I thought about how much I loved Grandfather, and about how much I loved Mom and Dad. Then I took a deep breath and chanted, "Help me, Mother Earth. Help me, Wakan Tanka."

I held the sacred feather above Peter's head. I knew I should pray in Lakota, the language of my people, the language of my grandfather, the real language of my mother. But I couldn't because I only knew a few words.

I was stopped then and there. I couldn't do it. Tears puddled in my eyes.

And then, like he was right next to me, I heard Grandfather singing. I suppose it was all in my imagination. It had to be, right? I guess so, but it sure seemed real. He sang the holiest Lakota song of all, "The Wakan Tanka." Then came the drums, booming deep and low. And then came the voices of the People—men, women, and children—singing together. The voices of my Lakota nation filled the room, the voices of my ancestors. The voices of Mother Earth and Father Sky. And the voices of all living beings in the great hoop of life. In my hour of need, they were with me, just like Grandfather always said they'd be.

English would have to do. I cleared my throat and prayed just as I heard Grandfather praying on top of the Empire State Building while the wind wolves howled around us.

"Wakan Tanka, please have mercy on me, please let my little brother live."

I shook the eagle feather. Drops sprayed on Peter's forehead, glistening where they fell like dew. I held my breath and waited. But Peter lay as still and small as before.

Nothing happened. I'd failed. I wasn't worthy enough. Maybe Mom was right. Maybe Grandfather lived in a dream world . . . and so did I. There was nothing more I could do. I was a complete failure—whatever did I think I was doing? I surrendered completely and threw myself across the bed and sobbed.

I don't know how long I lay there in the dark. Long enough to run out of tears and long enough to fall asleep. I know that seems like an amazingly stupid thing to do when nurses were crawling all over the place, but I couldn't help it. I was totally exhausted. I had given up. I was spent. I'd had a long day. The longest of my life.

But after all the crying, the tension sort of drained out of me. I went limp as a dishrag. So I just lay there, gritting my teeth at the absolutely hideous unfairness of everything. I felt sorry for Peter and I felt sorry for myself. Finally I quit sniffling and closed my eyes. I only wanted to rest a minute . . . I was so tired. And then it happened.

I was alone in a meadow. Behind me I could see mountains, all purple and white in the distance. An endless prairie, its tall grass swelling and rolling like the ocean, stretched before me. Above me a cloudless sky seemed so close I could jump up and grab it. Red and yellow flowers, heavy with pollen, and fat, buzzing bees swayed in the tall grass. I didn't know where I was, but I couldn't have cared less. It was a wonderful place.

A butterfly swooped past the tip of my nose, and I chased it. The tiny creature darted on the breeze, teasingly leading me on. Suddenly it vanished, and there in the air, so high it was barely a speck, was an eagle. Although the bird flew like the wind, I could somehow magically keep pace. I ran faster and faster. The cool air felt so good on my face.

A dot appeared on the horizon, gradually becoming larger as I approached. It was a snow-white tipi, sitting alone on the prairie like a shining island in a green sea. When I got closer, I saw a silver wisp curling from the smoke flaps. Someone was home. The eagle dove, dropping like a stone, and perched on the tipi's crossed lodgepoles.

I stopped, unsure of my next move. I wasn't scared though. Nothing in this place could ever be scary. The eagle screamed and beat its wings. "Okay," I said. I walked to the tipi, lifted the door flap and peered in. A human shape moved in the shadows on the far side of the campfire crackling in the fire pit. I ducked my head and went inside.

"We've been waiting for you, Feather," said a woman's soft voice.

I looked up in surprise and saw her. She was one of the People, and she was beautiful. She stood in front of me, tall, strong, and straight. Her beaded buckskin dress shimmered in the flickering light. Her black braids trimmed in white fur fell all the way to the ground. She had the kindest face I'd ever seen. Then she smiled at me. And that's when I felt it.

A power came out of her and rocked me like a gentle warm wave . . . a wave of loving kindness and compassion . . . and tremendous strength and wisdom. As it washed over me, I smelled the fresh scent of spring wildflowers, the cool forest soil and sun-kissed mountain rock. My heart fluttered and leapt up with a kind of gladness I'd never known before.

"Who are you?" I asked.

"Why, your mother," she answered.

"Wh-who?"

She laughed softly, the delicate sound, tinkling like the bells the Old Ones tied to the manes of their ponies. "Don't be afraid, Feather. I am your mother . . . the Earth."

"But . . . but . . ." I sputtered, "How did you know my name?"

She laughed again. "I know all my children. Come closer, my daughter."

I walked around the fire toward her. Just as I did a log shifted and fell, sending up a shower of blue sparks like fireworks. A little boy wearing fringed buckskins and a beaded headband peeked from behind the woman. His chubby fingers squeezed her hand tight. I froze when I got closer. Peter!

He smiled. "Hi, Fedder!" he called out cheerfully. His rosy cheeks were fat and full.

The woman reached out and held my hand, too. "Your prayer has been heard, Feather. Your path is straight and your heart is true. Go in peace and help your people."

"Peter will be okay? Really?"

She smiled ever so sweetly again and nodded. "Now I must send you back to your grandfather . . . with this." She kissed my cheek. "Go now, my child . . . and know you are worthy."

Shaking with happiness I rubbed my cheek. Her blessing was the most wonderful gift I'd ever received. I opened my mouth to thank her. I never got the chance.

Suddenly the ground buckled under my feet like a live animal. The woman, Peter, the fire, the tipi, and everything else including me, especially me, spun fiercely around as if tossed by a cyclone. Outside the eagle screamed. Then the whole world went black.

When I opened my eyes, I was lying on my stomach. My cheek felt wet, really wet. I lifted my head. It was drool. Drool was on my cheek. I'd been asleep.

Groggily I remembered I was at the hospital at the foot of Peter's bed. It hit me with great sadness that the beautiful woman was only a dream. I'd been so tired I had actually fallen asleep! How could I have fallen asleep when this had been my opportunity to do something for Peter? Grandfather was preparing me all day for this. What was wrong with me? How could I have fallen asleep! I was now totally furious with myself.

Muffled voices came from the hall. Dishes rattled and clanked in a cart. It sounded like the nurses were passing out dinner trays to the patients. "I gotta get out of here," I mumbled sleepily. I wondered how long I'd been out. I raised my arm and peered at the glowing green hands on my watch. Good, not long. Only ten or twelve minutes.

I shifted my other arm and noticed that the eagle feather was still in my hand. I rolled over onto my side. As I did I smelled the burnt sweetgrass smell on the feather. It reminded me of the woman in my dream. The scent was so powerful it brought her back to me, like she was there in the room.

I looked over at Peter. Somewhere above my head in the dark, his oxygen mask hissed away like a leaky inner tube. I was so upset I hadn't helped him. But I knew now that I had to somehow sneak out of the room. When I sat up the bed squeaked. I made a face and hoped no one heard. My next decision was crucial.

Making a clean getaway would be tough. I sat still for a minute and thought hard.

As I stared at the thin wedge of light coming from under the door, the bed shook. That didn't feel right. Peter and I were the only ones in the room. I held my breath and sat absolutely still. The bed wiggled again. I turned and squinted. It couldn't be.

"Hi, Fedder."

I yelled for joy. "Peter!"

Peter sat up in bed and yawned, as I flicked on the bedside lamp. He blinked in the light and propped the oxygen mask on top of his head like it was a pair of swimming goggles. Then he yawned and rubbed his eyes. Cute baby fat dimples covered his fists. I was so happy I was dizzy. I just stared at him with my mouth open for a second and then I swept him up in a big bear hug. When I finally let go, he wrinkled his forehead and frowned.

"Fedder . . . stop squeezing so hard," he giggled. "I have to tee-tee."

I whooped like a hyena and nearly fell off the bed.

About the same time, a herd of stampeding Nikes squeaked down the hall. The door burst open like it was pressurized. When the three nurses saw Peter and me, they froze in mid-charge. "Oh, my stars!" gasped the big blonde. Her two assistants stared over her shoulders in shock. "I'll g-go g-get the d-doctor," one of them stammered. She started to rush past the others, but swiveled around for another dazed look because she couldn't believe her eyes.

And that's when Hurricane Mom arrived. Shoving aside the gawking nurses like they were cardboard cutouts, she stormed into the room. Her eyes burned like black fire. She wagged a finger at me and shrieked: "Young lady, I warned you about—"

Well, that's as far as she got. She saw Peter smiling and sitting beside me. Or at least she thought she did. You could tell she couldn't believe it. At first she shook her head like she'd bumped it on something hard. Then one of the most amazing things I've ever seen happened. Mom's face was transformed into a dazzling kaleidoscope of emotions. It was like an exorcism or something! I laughed to myself. In a split second her expression changed from disbelief to surprise and then—when everything finally sank in—to . . . to, well, I guess the only thing you could call it was complete and total bliss.

"Peter!" she cried.

Peter bounced up on his knees. "Mommy!"

Tears poured down Mom's cheeks. She was sobbing big time as she held out her arms and grabbed him tight to her. "My baby, my baby!" And Peter thought *I* hugged him too hard! Mom climbed on the bed and hugged both of us like a vise. Rocking us in her arms, she threw her head back with her eyes shut tight and cried. Over and over she quietly murmured, "Thank you, God, thank you, God, thank you, God."

Somewhere in the middle of all this, everybody else rushed in and basically the whole room went nuts. To tell the truth, I'm surprised none of us were arrested for disturbing the peace.

After they hurriedly checked Peter over, the nurses slapped each other on the back like used car salesmen at a Las Vegas convention. Mrs. Silverman yahooed and kissed Mr. Houghton smack on the lips, who staggered backward groping for a chair. The doctor seemed to skid in through the door—that's how fast she had run to get here. She took one look at Peter, then amazingly deflated like a balloon, and took a deep breath from the oxygen mask herself. Dad and Emily hopped around doing some crazy tango to a loud chorus of "Omigosh! Omigosh!"

Grandfather stood in the doorway and enjoyed the show to the hilt. He wiped under his eyes with his bandanna and smeared his face paint.

"Tunkashila!" I called to him. "Everything's all right! He's okay!" I jumped off the bed and hugged him.

"He's okay now! Everything's going to be all right! Oh, Grandfather—Tunkashila—thank you! You did this. I know you did this! Peter's fine now!"

He put his hand on my face and smiled. "So he is, Takoja." Then he tousled Peter's hair.

Peter beamed up at him. "Pawpaw!"

Grandfather bent down on one knee to be level with Peter. "I've got something special for you, young man," he said as he gave Peter the wrapped present.

Peter clawed at the paper like a wild dog. When he saw the colorful box with its bold fire-engine image, he squealed. "A real fiya truck! Tank you, Pawpaw!"

Mom took Grandfather by the hand. "Dad, what . . . I mean . . . how did you do it?"

"Do what, my daughter?"

Mom kissed Peter right in the middle of his forehead. He giggled and tried to get away. She hugged him again. "This!"

Grandfather stood up. "I didn't heal him, Ann."

Mom looked puzzled. She sniffled and ran her fingers through her hair. "Wh-what do you mean? I don't understand. I thought—"

"The sacred gifts and traditions of his people saved him. Wakan Tanka and Mother Earth heard the prayers and sacrifices of a worthy medicine person. Someone strong, someone who walks the right path in her heart. But it wasn't me."

Well, when he said that, the room got real quiet. Emily, Dad, Mrs. Silverman, and the doctor gathered around to listen. Even the nurses piped down after Mrs. Silverman shushed them a couple of times.

Mom cleared her throat. "But you're a healer, right? And he was at death's door. I mean, I've never actually believed in your healing, not . . . not since Mother died anyway." She looked at the pipe cradled in Grandfather's arms. "I lost my faith the day the ambulance took her away." She reached out and gently stroked the pipe's eagle feather fan. Her voice sank to a whisper. "Now . . . now I don't know. Maybe some prayers are answered."

Suddenly she slid off the bed and threw her arms around Grandfather's neck. "Oh, Dad, I've been so . . . so bitter. So unfair. Can you ever forgive me?"

Grandfather patted her on the back. "Ann, there's nothing you could ever do to make my love less than total. There's nothing for me to forgive. I've always been proud of you. Always."

Mrs. Silverman blew her nose into a big wad of Kleenex and daubed her eyes. "What a family this is!"

Grandfather tilted his hat back on his head. "Ann, there's only one thing I ask of you."

Mom went and sat by Peter. She looked like a different person. She almost glowed. "Anything, Dad. Anything."

Grandfather picked his sacred medicine feather up off the bed where I'd dropped it when Peter woke up. Then he held it in front of Mom. "Do you think maybe you could remember the path of the heart? The sacred path of your Lakota people?"

Mom nodded and sighed. "After today my life starts over. I promise. What you just did changed my whole—"

"Once again, I did nothing, my daughter. Nothing other than to prepare the way. The healer you seek is here." Grandfather slowly turned and offered me the medicine feather. As I stood there with my mouth open, Dad made a little low whistle between his teeth, and Emily clamped her hand over her mouth and started to do her breathing trick. Mrs. Silverman nudged the doctor with her elbow and whispered, "What did I tell you!"

I looked at Grandfather, unable to move or say anything. My heart thumped. Finally I took the feather.

Grandfather raised the medicine pipe over my head. "Feather is our new medicine person. She's our young healer." He turned slowly as he proudly announced this to everyone in the room.

Mom put her hands to her lips in astonishment, and I noticed her fingers were trembling. She stared at Grandfather, thunderstruck. Her voice was really hoarse now. "You mean *she's* the one who—" She broke off in mid-sentence as she watched Peter happily rolling his fire truck over the blankets.

Grandfather laughed quietly. "Yes, it's true. It was she who did this. All I did was lead the way."

Mom looked at me like she was really seeing me for the first time. "Oh, Feather. I'm so sorry . . . I've been so wrong about . . . about everything." Then she smiled at me, something she hadn't done in months. "I love you, honey, so much."

"I know, Mom. I love you, too." It felt as though I was seeing my mother for the first time, too. And then I smiled. Like a thousand suns.

CHAPTER EIGHTEEN

Well, that's how it all happened. Peter is okay now. Completely cured, in fact. The doctor said she'd never seen anything like it in twenty years of practicing medicine in New York City. For his part Peter's back at his old job. Bugging me. Every day after he gets home from kindergarten, he spends most of his free time watching the cartoon channel or running around the apartment like a maniac with his fire engine blaring. That thing is a lot noisier than I thought it would be. I don't know who it annoys more, Mom or me. One day I swear I'm going to hide the batteries. Grandfather seems kind of fond of all the racket. He says it sounds happy. Loud but happy.

Emily is doing great since her acting debut at the hospital. Broadway definitely awaits a new star. She isn't terrified of life the way she was before, although she's more of a drama queen than ever. It's kind of her trademark, I guess. And I love this about her. She took White Buffalo Calf Girl to her history class the other day. They're doing a unit on Native Americans and she filled everybody in on the myths and legends of the Lakota people. I definitely would've liked to hear her spin on that!

Mrs. Silverman is around even more than usual. To tell the truth Grandfather and she are kind of dating, I think. They're always going off to the movies, or bookstores, or a museum . . . or the top of the Empire State Building . . . or the zoo. They're like teenagers. Well, almost. They sure do make a cute couple, although I'm getting pretty sick and tired of blueberry cheesecake for dessert. If they do get married, I better be the maid of honor.

Mrs. Chen still runs her store in the Village . . . and probably will for another fifty years. Grandfather and I eat lunch with her every Saturday. Mrs. C. and I have really become good friends. She's teaching me all about herbs, natural medicines, how to recognize good antiques—and how to make a killer pizza. She's something else! If anything I suspect she may actually be getting younger. She's even talking about opening a jazz coffee bar in Tribeca!

I haven't seen Mrs. Green lately. I still have the odd quarter necklace she gave me—what Grandfather called a "stone amulet." I keep it around the neck of the buffalo Grandfather gave me that day. Whenever I'm out, I keep my eyes peeled for Mrs. Green. But I won't play hooky any more either to trail after her when I think I've spotted her . . . that's for sure. I'm not worried, though. Some day when I least expect it, there she'll be, standing in the crosswalk right in front of my cab. And I'll be so happy when that day comes.

I just want to thank her. After all, Mrs. Green's an integral piece of the puzzle of that wonderful day. And I'll always be grateful for her. And I'm grateful for every part that contributed to the indispensable web of that day, as Grandfather always says about the great web of life. That's how I feel about all the wonderful people and animals of that special day when Peter came back to life and I discovered who I was.

Only I really know I could not have done it without Grandfather, my great teacher, and the wisest person I know. Maybe I'll become a doctor myself one day, a different kind, one who knows medicine but one who also knows the old ways and can help people. That's what I've been kind of thinking about lately, ever since that night at the hospital with Peter.

Meanwhile Dad is back in South America for another semester. He finally got tenure and he's on top of the world. This summer when school's out, he promised to take me to Cambodia for six weeks on an archeological dig. He says we need to see more of each other in the future. I definitely agree.

Mom has changed the most. Since Peter got well it's like she's a completely different person. For one thing she left her old firm and is practicing law on her own now. She opened her own office and she's doing great. Just the other night she was on CNN. She had a case before the State Supreme Court in Albany representing some Mohawk people who were trying to get some of their tribal lands back. And she won!

You know, it's funny. Even though she's working harder than ever, it seems like she has more time for Peter, Grandfather, and me. Personally I think it's because she's not, you know, half a person any more. She's whole because she feels so rewarded, like she told me one night, what with her important work and all. And there's another thing. Since the hospital she's wanted to learn more about her Indian heritage. Well, you can imagine how that makes Grandfather feel. And she's taking better care of herself, too. She started an exercise program and she's been eating right and doing yoga.

In fact I need to log off right now because she just came in from her afternoon run and she wants to visit.

We talk constantly now. It's like you can't shut her up. The only way I can explain it is that for the first time in our lives we're . . . well, friends.

Oh! Wait! She just told me that she saw an eagle soaring over Central Park today when she was exercising. Man, you should see the expression on her face. She looks all spacey like one of those people who hand out weird pamphlets on street corners. Mom says she knows the eagle is important to our people, but she's forgotten all the old campfire tales she heard as a child. She wants me to help her remember. She wants me to tell her a story. And the supremely great news is she just stuck her head back in the room and said, "And by the way, you're not grounded anymore!"

Well, that's totally cool. Mrs. Green and I are off the hook.

And, hey, I almost forgot. I didn't mention what happened that night at the hospital after everything calmed down. When he was alone with only Peter and me, Grandfather held another ceremony with his medicine pipe. He even let Peter hold it! When it was all over, he gave me my new name . . . my special Lakota name that I'll keep forever. He says that after I come into my full power as a medicine woman, I can finally reveal it. In the meantime, whenever he gets the chance, he's teaching me all about the traditional sacred rites of our people and what it means to be a healer. It's been an awesome experience. But that's another story.

THE END